Achs

The Poet and Other Poems

SALZWASSER
VERLAG

Achsa W. Sprague

The Poet and Other Poems

Reprint of the original, first published in 1865.

1st Edition 2022 | ISBN: 978-3-75259-042-5

Verlag (Publisher): Salzwasser Verlag GmbH, Zeilweg 44, 60439 Frankfurt, Deutschland
Vertretungsberechtigt (Authorized to represent): E. Roepke, Zeilweg 44, 60439 Frankfurt, Deutschland
Druck (Print): Books on Demand GmbH, In de Tarpen 42, 22848 Norderstedt, Deutschland

POEMS.

THE POET

AND

OTHER POEMS.

BY

ACHSA W. SPRAGUE.

BOSTON:
WILLIAM WHITE AND CO.,
158 WASHINGTON STREET.
1865.

ADVERTISEMENT.

The contents of this volume include but a portion of the Poems placed in the hands of the compiler for publication. There remains material more than sufficient for another volume of the size of the present. It has been a task of some difficulty to make a selection, where none were found devoid of merit. But the reluctance that was felt in excluding much that seemed valuable, has been partially overcome by the hope that a more complete edition of the poetical writings of Miss Sprague will be called for at some future day, when the present disturbed condition of the country shall be overpast. Meanwhile, it has been the aim of the compiler to include in this book enough of poetical merit, and variety in the shorter pieces, to make it an acceptable offering to the many friends of the lamented author, and to the reading public.

In justice to the author, it ought to be stated, that the long poem, and the greater part of the "Miscellaneous Poems" included in this collection, were composed (together with many others still unpublished) but a short time previous to her death, and while she was convalescing from severe illness. The rapidity with which they were then written, or dictated to a ready writer, with the sudden relapse and closely following death of Miss Sprague, deprived these pieces, beyond doubt, of that revision and consequent perfection in form, which they would ultimately have received from her own hand, before being given to the public.

Her poems were written, in general, as relaxations from more active duties, or, in periods of imperfect health, as a mode of relief for an intense mental activity. A good many short pieces were published in various newspapers, at the time they were first written, but she had taken no steps toward publishing anything in a book form. The present collection, though containing imperfections and occasional harshnesses which under different circumstances might have been avoided, is sent to the world with a confidence that it possesses merits, both of thought and expression, that will well repay a perusal.

SOUTH READING, VERMONT,
May 1, 1864.

CONTENTS.

THE POET.

MISCELLANEOUS POEMS.

EARLY POEMS.

THE unexpected and untimely death of Miss A. W. SPRAGUE, in the summer of 1862, brought a pang of sorrow to many hearts. And there are many still, scattered up and down through fifteen States of the Union, who hold her in loving remembrance, though, in the whirlpool of revolution and civil war that has since convulsed the nation, many a fair reputation has gone down to speedy oblivion. During a brief public career she had travelled extensively, and had everywhere made for herself troops of friends. From Maine to Missouri, from Montreal to Baltimore, there are earnest, truth-loving men and women who will not soon forget the impression they received, as well from her conversation as her pnblic discourses.

Miss Sprague was chiefly known to the world as a trance lecturer under what claimed to be spirit-influence. In this capacity she had for several years been an active laborer. A pioneer advocate of the Spiritual Philosophy in New England, she was also a devoted friend of every philanthropic and reformatory enterprise of the time, ranking with the best of her class, — with Emma Hardinge, Cora Hatch, and a few others, — in catholicity of spirit, in large views, and earnest, telling speech. Although speaking in the interest of a faith generally unpopular, and involved in no slight degree in crudities, extravagance, and quackery, she was herself neither fool nor fanatic. And while the reality of spiritual intercourse, the nearness of the angel-world to ours, the certain assurance of unending, ever-progressive life beyond the grave, were themes upon which she often dwelt, she loved most to forget all party watchwords, and, ignoring shallow distinctions of sect or class, push out into the broad realms of truth, regarding hearer and theme alike from the stand point simply of enlightened humanity. In this spirit, she did not fail to criticise with severity any attempt or tendency she discovered among Spiritualists, to erect the new teachings into a dogma or a ritual. She was wont to speak of these teachings as a spiritual philosophy, and chose to regard them as constituting a new dispensation of religious truth to man. A movement now in its infancy, but destined to extend itself far and wide till it encompassed the earth. Though an advance from all previous revelations, the present was but the dawn of the New Era. It was the day of small things, — mediums were imperfect, conditions unfavorable. Like the seers of all ages, she saw and reported that there are new and fresher gospels waiting to be given, whenever mankind shall be fitted to receive them. She caught glimpses of that illimitable ocean of truth, unfathomable by human thought, but which some bold Columbus shall yet disclose to man.

> This does but herald brighter things to come,
> Before whose beauty shall the earth sit dumb.
>
> . . . .
>
> And known at last shall be God's great unknown,
> And man, unshamed, shall claim it as his own.
>
> The Poet, Scene III.

She taught a perennial inspiration — a stream ever gushing forth from the eternal fountain, whether called for or not. It seemed a great poverty of manhood in the human race, that it should have had no model man for eighteen hundred years. There was need of a great religious teacher to do for this age what Jesus did for his. And might it not be that we had impaired our ability to receive new revelations, by looking too closely and too implicitly upon the old? She said: We find the fresh footsteps of Deity always in our path, but such is our traditional timidity that we dare not trust the evidence of our senses, and recognize them as such, till we go and compare them with the footprints of the olden time. But while we are busy thus comparing them the great God has himself passed on.

Her influence as a public speaker was remarkable. Always deeply in earnest, elegant and forcible in her style of speaking, equally removed from extravagance on the one hand and tameness on the other, she rose not unfrequently to a chaste and noble eloquence. She spoke habitually upon the highest themes, with a scope and vigor of thought, and a fertility of illustration rarely equalled. Her speaking was an inspiration. She possessed that power of the true orator — of uplifting those she addressed into higher regions of thought and feeling. Some of her periods were very grand, and will not soon be forgotten by those who heard them. Swayed by a pure moral enthusiasm, as she advanced with her subject, the hearer was borne along upon the tide of a robust and persuasive speech. Her manner, meanwhile, partook of the elevation of her thought, and enforced it by appropriate and vigorous action. There was nothing of rant or theatric display, no sacrifice of womanly delicacy; but a simple yet queenly dignity in excellent keeping with the discourse. No studied elegance of posture or movement, but a native majesty of presence, the natural expression of the body possessed and animate with the informing soul. In Vermont, which was her earliest lecturing field, her hold upon the public mind was very deep. Multitudes who never distinctively accepted spiritual intercourse as a fact, were wont to listen to her with unaffected delight. Though prized most in places where she was best known, yet, wherever she went, she was sure of overflowing houses. It was common to see people at her meetings in the smaller towns, who had come eight, ten, or fifteen miles to hear "the preaching woman."

To the esteem in which she was held for her merits as a lecturer, was added, at least in the vicinity of her home, the interest that attached to the story of her life. Her youth had been one long struggle with poverty and suffering. Remarkable from her earliest years for an eager, insatiable thirst after knowledge, the circumstances of her family forbade any save the most limited gratification to this her ruling desire. There was a large family of children, and the old tragedy of Want and Have was daily enacted in the home. Sickness came there, — a frequent guest. Mr. Sprague, the father, a man gifted by nature with uncommon powers of mind, had long been the victim of an uncontrollable appetite for strong drink. Achsa, his six child, was a sprightly girl, fond of being much in the open air. Opportunities for education were scanty, even for a sparsely-populated country district. A common school of some sort held its sessions during six months of the year. Thither she went, whenever the domestic affairs of the family would permit, until she was twelve, when she began teaching, first in a family in an adjoining town, and the succeeding summer in a common school. Before this, and while she was yet a pupil, she had been used by her teachers to conduct lower classes in school. From thence till she was twenty, she was teaching the larger part of the time when her health was sufficient, having taught in all eighteen terms. Meanwhile, she attended at an academy for a term and a half, which completed the small debt she owed to school education. In private she had doubtless improved every resource to extend the boundaries of her knowledge. There were no circulating libraries within reach, and little access to good books; but she must have missed no opportunity during this period, of borrowing from individuals whenever practicable. Still, all that could be obtained in this way must have come far short of satisfying that hungry intellect. Society of persons of superior cultivation there was little or none, though the father, in his better hours, felt an honest pride in his daughter, and knew how to encourage her aspiring and ambitious nature.

But now there came an experience so dark and sorrowful as to make all her previous life, checkered by clouds as it was, seem but pure sunshine in comparison. Over-mastering disease laid its heavy hand upon this rare and promising girl. She entered upon the terrible discipline of a seven years' sickness — a period full of agony and gloom, but destined to prove in its results of exceeding import to her future life. Gradual in its approaches as the shades of night fall upon the earth, her disease knew no pause till its victim lay helpless before its ravages. It was of scrofulous nature, and first settled in her joints, rendering them almost useless. Medical assistance brought no relief. For a while the youthful hopes of the sufferer bore up cheerily, and through the aid of crutches she continued to teach for a term or two. But every resource failing, as month after month passed on and she grew steadily worse, hope seemed to fade away and give place to a settled despair. Not the despair that trembles at the view of death, but the hopelessness of living on, of dragging out life in perpetual suffering and helplessness. The "Early Poems" printed in this volume, and mostly written during the earlier stages of her sickness, sufficiently portray the state of her feelings at this period, and the load of anguish that weighed down her spirit. Every stanza seems measured by the heavy heart-throbs of the writer. Before her sickness her aspiring mind had doubtless planned for itself a broad field of future activity and usefulness, and it was with difficulty that she could bring herself to renounce at once and forever all that young imagination had painted in fairest colors.

But as the darkness deepened to midnight, and the last hope went out with the passage of weary years, she prayed wildly for death; — begged and implored that she might not longer cumber the earth, a burden to her friends and to herself. "Speak not of *dreaded* death," — she afterwards wrote, — "I wooed the stern Archer as a friend. And yet he passed me by, and, passing, pierced some happy heart that loved to live. I might have borne the pain (perhaps I might), but oh, the dreary thought of living in vain! Year after year to come and go, and yet to leave no trace that I had ever been, save added wrinkles on my mother's brow! To live, and yet not live; to die, and yet not die; to feel the restless thought, the wish to do, the yearning for some *active life* forever struggling in my soul, and yet to be a captive in my prison-cell! no power to save, and none to roll away the stone from that dark, *living tomb*, and set me free!" Her spirit panted for action. She could not bear and yet be still, but wildly wrestled with her fate in those sad hours. Her disease, though painful in all its stages, was of a nature that left the mind free to range at will and contemplate the activities of life, which, in view of her enfeebled physical condition, seemed to mock her own blighted hopes and crushed aspirations. Cut off from all bodily exercise, her mental faculties became preternaturally active, so that it was an agony to think, and at the same time impossible not to do so. Waves of thought and feeling came and went, and swept her soul like ocean tides. As the billows of the sea when raised by tempests, rush to the land, and with their long roll beat the shores, so the waves of thought, she said, seemed to lash the shores of her being, and beat, beat, against the frail bark of life till it seemed ready to go to pieces before their ever-greatening force.

But relief came at last to her sufferings, and in a way little expected. In "The Angel's Visit," at the end of this volume, her own pen has described the manner of her release, and the aims and purposes with which she went forth once more to mingle in the active world. This is not the place to enter upon a philosophical discussion as to the nature of the occult influence there operating, nor would it be profitable, since the subject must be finally left, as it still exists in the mind of the writer, an unsolved enigma. Whatever may have been the agency in her cure,— and wonderful it certainly was,—no one who knew her, ever imputed dishonesty to her, or intention to deceive. It required some severe mental struggles before she was persuaded fully to trust the mysterious influence that was more and more clearly manifesting itself. But in it was her only hope; and following out a course of treatment prescribed by the invisible intelligences, she was in six months restored to comparative health. Meanwhile, it began to be intimated to her by the same influence, that there was an important public work waiting for her to do, — a work for humanity required of her in return for the service she had herself received; that this was the result had in view from the beginning. She was put in training for public speaking, detailed instructions being given, and exercises prescribed, such as it is difficult to suppose could proceed from her own mind. Her thoughts were at the same time turned strongly towards religious and ethical subjects, and, as her health improved, she was moved to write frequently upon the same. Gradually it was broken to her that she must take the field as a public speaker. At first she had a strong repugnance to anything of the kind; but finally, after some sacrifice of feeling, she acquiesced in what many considerations, and especially gratitude, seemed to demand of her. A decision that she never regretted. This was in the spring of 1854. She gave her first public discourse at South Reading, Vermont, on the 16th of July of the same year. From that day onward till her death, at Plymouth, Vermont, July 6th, 1862, her life was full of busy work. What that work was we need not rehearse here, nor tell the joy she found in her new vocation. With a brief allusion to a few of the less familiar aspects of her career as a lecturer, we will pass to a conclusion of these remarks. Those who knew her best, can testify with what willing earnestness she labored, speaking, much of the time, from three to five or six times a week, and travelling constantly, in order to give evening lectures in places out of the way of her regular Sunday appointments. There was always a large demand upon her services, and she was reluctant to refuse calls so long as there was a prospect of doing any good.

From the beginning of her public life, she had felt an earnest desire to speak to the inmates of the Prisons. Her sympathies were strongly moved in behalf of this class of persons, often quite as much the victims of society, as characterized by any special depravity of nature. At Providence and Philadelphia, permission was obtained at her solicitation, to address the prisoners, and a standing invitation extended to renew her visits at any time. At Boston she was less successful in getting access to the Charlestown State Prison, though her efforts were seconded by several members of the legislature, then in session. In Philadelphia, she went several times to the penitentiary, for private conference with the females confined there. Sometimes she came away quite disheartened from these visits. "It is sad," she wrote, "to look upon such an abandoned class of people, sad to to see their condition, both of mind and body; and I sometimes wonder why I wish to go among them, when, at best, one can do so little good. But somehow my soul cries out for the privilege of doing that little, at the expense of the dark scenes that the lifting of the curtain must reveal to me." Wherever she journeyed, she was accustomed to give frequent benefit-lectures, the proceeds to be applied for the relief of the poor, and for other charitable purposes. Many also were the cases of individual destitution in cities, that she sought out and helped to relieve. She had herself drank deep of poverty's cup, from earliest childhood, and knew well its bitter taste. Meeting once at Troy, N. Y., Laura Edmonds, daughter of the judge, giving free sittings for the investigation of spiritual manifestations, she is seized with regret that she cannot go about the country lecturing in like manner without money and without price. "But, ah me! I am poor," she says. "Still, I never have a stated price, but leave it to the means or generosity of the people to do by me as they think proper. I should like it if I had money, that I might do more good. Yet I cannot make Spiritualism a stepping-stone to wealth; it seems like debasing the most beautiful things."

It is easy to see that her sympathies widened year by year, and her mind liberalized as she came into larger contact with the world. She was too large-natured to live shut up to the influence of a single idea. She warmly interested herself in the chief reforms and humanitary movements of the day. Her discourses, while losing nothing of their former spirit, grew more direct and practical in their character, as from a broader observation she studied the actual condition of society and its deepest needs. She became acquainted, either personally or through their writings, with many of the leading minds of the age, — with the strong, earnest soul of Theodore Parker, with the quaint wisdom of Emerson, with the impassioned poetry of Mrs. Browning, whose Aurora Leigh was long a book of especial significance to her. Her poems, written both before and since the outbreak of the rebellion, attest the patriotic interest she always felt in republican ideas. That last printed before her death, she inscribed to the Union Volunteers, dedicating it, with her deepest gratitude and earnest prayers, "to the brave and loyal hearts offering their lives at the Shrine of Liberty."

As respects the Poems contained in this volume, little needs be said here. The world will judge of the degree of merit they possess. They can never, of course, have that interest for a stranger, as for those who knew the author, and saw the excellence of her character in public and private. To such, these poems, though genuine products of the writer's individuality, are but chance bubbles on the stream of a life, deep, pure, earnest, and strong. Characteristic, and suggestive of much, they are but the chip of granite from the top of Mount Washington. And there is reason to believe that these are unimportant, as compared with what would have been produced had the author been spared to reach the full maturity of her powers. Though from an early age she had occasionally attempted the writing of poetry, she had but just entered upon her career as an author. She was writing extensively, with no special view to publication, and regarded these productions for the most part as experiments and exercises in the art of writing. They should be judged, therefore, somewhat as the juvenile efforts of authors are estimated, — not only for what they are, but for the better promise they contain. The rapidity with which they were composed, is not the least remarkable feature in their history. "The Poet," containing, as written, over

4,600 lines, was finished within three weeks from the time of its commencement, and actually required not more than seventy-two consecutive hours in being committed to paper. "The Child of Destiny," a dramatic poem of about 3,000 lines, still unpublished, was completed in five and a half days from its commencement. Such facility in composition, it is thought, is hardly surpassed in the whole history of literary composition. From two to three hundred lines were usually thrown off at an evening's sitting. Sometimes, in a state of high mental exaltation, she would walk the room, dictating for an amenuensis to write, whose ready pencil not unfrequently found it difficult to keep pace with her rapid recitation. This extraordinary development of writing, began in January, 1862, as she was recovering from a severe illness at Oswego, N. Y. Her health continued slowly to improve until the first of May following, when she returned to her home in Vermont, as it proved, to die. Her physical strength was still low; but she continued to write, when engaged with a long poem, often at the rate of five hundred lines per day. She seemed impelled by an irresistible power to undertake new projects, and then to finish what had been begun. On the 10th of June, in a letter to a friend, she said that her health was decidedly better, that she was getting much engaged in writing, that it rested her, and that she enjoyed it as a pastime. Near the end of the month she rode to Rutland and back in a carriage, from which time she declined rapidly, until a violent brain fever set in, and, on the 6th of July, the last earthly change had taken place.

Her death seems untimely, and many found it hard to acquiesce in an event that removed one so young, so active, and so anxious to do good, while the world needed her so much. This feeling was heightened by the impression that she needlessly overworked herself, and did not prudently husband her strength. She used up life too rapidly, in violation of physiological law. She knew no moderation in work, and did not often take counsel of prudence, so long as there was a call upon her services. It seems scarcely less than madness to attempt such mental labor as she performed during the last months of her life, and with physical strength so much reduced. Indeed, there is reason to think, that from the time of her first sickness, before her mediumship, her mental activity had been excessive, and incompatible with a permanently healthy condition of body. Various causes conspired to prolong this tendency, till it was manifest at last as an inflamed intellectualism. Be this as it may, she died after all, perhaps, in a way that it befitted her to die. To put a restraint upon the mobility of the mind's powers, it must be remembered, is precisely the thing that people of her intensely active temperament find it hardest to do. Could such an eager, ambitious soul bear to outlive its activity, bear to see its faculties fail one by one, and sink into imbecility and second childishness? Does not the eagle that is wont to mount to the sun on free and joyous wing, beat the bars of his prison-cage, when captured, till he dies, spurning life on such terms? So our friend, having once tasted the joy that comes of the large, free exercise of our noblest powers, could never again content herself with the dull, plodding life that suffices for most of us. Or, from a higher plane of thought, might she not have answered one who thought to chide her for her want of moderation: I am set at my post, like a soldier, for a certain duty. Like a true soldier, I will stand at my post. If danger and death confront me there, I will meet them as I ought, cheerfully; I shall never, never desert my place, or betray the trust.

She had a lofty ambition, — daring yet pure. In the windows of the picture-shops, the reader may some time have seen a print illustrating Longfellow's spirited little poem — "Excelsior." A youth with outspread banner in his hand, is struggling up the slippery ascent of a huge Alpine mountain. Above him rise the steeps of mighty glaciers, their summits hid in clouds. Darkness is coming on, — the last rays of the setting sun gild the snowy peaks far, far above. Just beneath, in a little vale, lies a hamlet, and from a cottage by the wayside has come out an old man, whose silver hairs speak of wisdom and experience, who is warning the youth not to proceed further, cautioning him against the madness of attempting to scale the mountain. Near to the old man stands his daughter, with shining ringlets falling upon her neck, who modestly but earnestly adds her entreaties to the sage admonitions of the sire. But the youth is deaf to both; and standing proudly upon the cliff above them, with one hand he displays his banner and its glittering inscription, and with the other points upward to the dizzy heights that rear themselves aloft in wild grandeur. No dangers can daunt, no appeals move him. No cheerful light of blazing hearths can detain him from his self-imposed task. In the cold twilight he presses on through a waste of drifting snows. Next morning he is found by the pious monks of the hospital upon the mountain-top, "lifeless but beautiful," with the cherished banner closely wrapped about his stiffened form. I am strangely reminded of this picture whenever I think of our departed friend, — her indomitable, ever forward-pressing spirit, and her early fall. Its significance is, of course, in its symbolic meaning. It is the consecration of youthful heroism, — a heroism deterred by no obstacle, seduced by no blandishments, and intent only upon the execution of a lofty purpose. It is the self-immolation of genius at the shrine of a pure ambition.

Somebody has said that it might be well for all poets, if nothing more were known of their lives than appears in their poetry. This may be true of such as Edgar A. Poe, of whom it was especially said, but it is not true of her whose name stands upon the title-page of this volume. No one, in extending his knowledge of her, ever had occasion to lessen his esteem for her as a person, or accept a lower estimate of her character.

I have not sought to pass an indiscriminate eulogium upon her; but want of space compels me rather to pass over in silence many admirable traits. Hence I may not speak of her steadfast earnestness of purpose, her tireless industry, her indomitable energy, —

whether teaching school on crutches, or rising from a sick-bed to fulfil an appointment to lecture; her ardent love of Nature, that opened every sense to the perception of the beautiful and sublime in mountain and lake, in stream and dell, in woods and waterfall. She was a true child of nature, direct and simple in her manners, and impatient of the artificiality and formal etiquette of fashionable society. In her public ministrations she was earnest yet liberal, zealous but tolerant. With a large vein of mysticism in her composition, she would have the truths of Religion made clear to the understanding also. She left a name upon which detraction sought in vain to find a blot; and though much admired, she had too much good sense to be spoiled by flattery. Beginning life a victim of poverty, in youth a child of suffering, she was lastly, in her adult years, a dispenser of benefits to many a grateful mind. The writer of these pages first made her acquaintance when he was a young collegian, full of the conceits of knowledge without the reality. Heretofore inclined to despise the intellectual capacities of the gentler sex, she quite revolutionized his estimate of woman. It was a surprise to meet so much originality of character, so much mental vigor and independence, where one was wont to expect only subserviency to low social standards and fashionable follies. She was the noblest woman it has been my lot to know, and the impress of her spirit is left too deep upon my memory ever to be obliterated. Whatever changes may come, however low I may fall, I can never quite forget that, in the impressible years of my youth, I knew, and walked for a while in tho radiance of, a pure and lofty character. And now that she has closed her earthly career, and is added to that ever-greatening host that have passed beyond the dark valley, she is well entitled to the hospitality and fellowship of those master spirits "who have labored to impregnate the minds of men with bold and lofty conceptions, who have taught the men of their generation to crave after the unseen, to pine after the ideal, and rise above the visible world of sense." M. E. G.

THE POET.

THE POET.

SCENE I.

An hour before sunset. A thickly-shaded bower in the forest. Glimpses of the ocean through the trees. A POET sitting in an attitude of dejection, with torn fragments of paper containing pencilled snatches of songs scattered about. Thinks aloud.

POET.

MY burning thought leaps up in rhyme,
And sets itself to many a chime;
Like deep, long-hidden, glowing fires,
Through all my soul it yearns, aspires,
And worships at some fairer shrine
Than here I see,—aye, more divine.

I cannot bear this thought that burns,
And ever so intensely turns
To some strange altar deep within,
And strives my outer self to win;

It makes me lonely in the crowd,
O'er all that's fair I see a shroud,
The things of life seem poor and vain,
I have no wish to taste again.
There's discord in each tone I hear,
For from the soul's deep-hidden sphere
There ever comes a voice to me,
That says, "We call, we call to thee."
What fills me with such great unrest?
What aching void is in my breast?
What clouds of darkness and of night?
What yearning for a purer light?
That, sick at heart, I turn away
Still more and more, day after day,
From what the world calls bright and fair,
And feel 'tis vain,—for me no share;
From what seems great and good to men,
To sit me down alone again,
And listen to the ceaseless din
Of elements at work within,
That seem to struggle in their power,
Each one for victory in its hour;
And hear the deep and solemn tone
In some strange temple grave and lone,
That stands within my inmost soul,
Whose anthems ever ceaseless roll;
And strive to enter at its gate,

No more to watch and weary wait,
And find the beautiful within,
And cleanse myself from every sin.

What leaps like lightning through my soul,
Sudden and swift beyond control,
As if Jove's hand its bolt had sent,
Or some half-God a power had lent,
Or, like Prometheus' stolen fire,
In pity at my long desire,
Then dies away, its source unknown,
And leaves me still more sad and lone; —
Aye, leaves the weary, wasting pain,
That preys till it shall come again?

[*A pause*

I would do something worthy life, —
I'm weary of this fruitless strife, —
Something that lends a golden ray,
Like sunset to the parting day.
Immortal longings in me rise,
An earnestness that never dies,
To smite the rock within my soul,
And make its living waters roll.
Are there no powers within me deep,
Half-latent, rising from their sleep,
By virtue of their innate strength
To find an utterance at length?

Consuming fires within me burn,
Whichever way my soul may turn,
Still scorching, eating out the heart,
Till thought becomes a fiery dart
To pierce my spirit through with pain,
Until I pray for rest again.
Fires long pent up within the earth,
Though cramped, restrained, will yet have birth;
Some Etna or Vesuvius wakes,
Or Earth unto its centre shakes.
Thought pent within the human mind,
At last its inborn powers shall find,
And mightier that so long it's lain
Bound by a hidden, potent chain,
It bursts its bands at last with might,
And springs to meet the morning light.

Rouse up, O soul within my soul!
That yearns for some mysterious goal;
Hast thou not strength to burst away,
And feel thy power and hold thy sway?
Droop not so sadly every wing!
I hear thy plaintive murmuring:
Speak not so mournfully of light,
As if 'twere shrouded in the night;
But find thy might, and burst forth strong:
Thy time has come, thou'st waited long.

Call up rich powers, thyself to speak,
And stand erect — no more the weak;
Let thy best thought find burning word
By which the human soul is stirred.
Burst forth, O soul! why may not song
And outward speech to thee belong?
Why may not some free utterance take
The place of thy long silence? Break
The seal from off the inner shrine,
And breathe in words its thoughts divine!
Burst every chain! at last be free!
Give forth the thoughts that burn in thee!
Take some rich harp, its numbers try,
And sing thyself, or, striving, die!

Spirit of Poesy.

I HAVE heard thy deep prayer, and the answer is given,
I will breathe through thy soul like a voice from the heaven;
I will tune every string of thy spirit's deep lyre,
Till it thrills and it speaks of thy soul's hidden fire;
I will pour through its cells such a power and a strength,
That each thought shall leap up in its armor at length,
And shall rush forth to mingle in songs of the earth,
And thrill through the mind where rich thoughts have their birth.

I will whisper to thee with a voice small and still,
Till each fibre shall tremble, each heart-chord shall
thrill,
Till the Spirit of Beauty looks up where she smiled,
And wraps in her mantle and claims thee her child;
And she clothes in sweet music the words as they fall,
Till they bind with a spell the true spirits of all.
I will touch with my wand the god-Genius that sleeps
Far down in thy spirit, far down in its deeps,
Till he wakes from his slumbers, leaps up in his power,
And acknowledges thee thrice baptized in that hour.
He shall touch thee anew from his altar of flame,
With the fire of his power and the light of his name,
Till in strength thou shalt rise, and his spirit and fire
Shall accomplish for thee all thy heart's long desire.
I will bathe thee in beauty, I'll bathe thee in love,
Till thy voice has a tone like the angels above,
Till thine eye speaks the fire that is burning within,
And it beams and it beckons all others to win;
Till thy lips have a purpose, a strength, and a power,
All the wealth of thy soul over others to shower,
And thy words strangely thrill through the depths of
the heart,
Long after the breath from these lips shall depart.
I will take up thy soul like a lute, and each string
With melody soft 'neath my fingers shall ring;
I will sweep o'er thy heart like a harp with its chords,

Till each string has a voice, and each tone breathes in
words.
I will touch the rich keys with my long-practised
hand;—
It shall be like an organ, prophetic and grand;
It shall wail as in grief, it shall speak as in joy,
Be a promise of glory no night can destroy.
It shall rise into grandeur, or sink into pain,
Then sweep and reëcho, and echo again.
I will pour o'er thy soul all my magic divine:
I have heard thy deep prayer, and my gifts shall be
thine.

Poet.

Whence came that voice, those burning words?
They seemed from earth or sky;
At times so very far away—
Again so closely nigh.

What art thou? Spirit of the wind?
Queen-fairy of this wood?
Or Genius of these summer waves?—
I'd reach thee if I could.

Thy voice gave answers to my prayers;—
Oh, could desires take word,

From out my yearning soul would come
  The very tones I heard!

And have I thought until my brain,
  Bewildered, weaves this spell,
And airy fancy plays me false,
  And says, "All shall be well"?

Oh, speak again! if aught beside
  Gave forth that tone of heaven.
Speak! give me proof, that gifts like these,
  To me can, *will* be given!

Spirit of Poesy.

I am the Spirit of Poesy,
  I am the Soul of Song,
I have waited and listened to thee, soul,
  Waited and listened so long.

Deep in thy spirit I've seen the germ—
  Germ of a power divine;
I have watched and I've waited its growth, soul,
  Waited to call it to mine.

Fed by thy tears and thy trials dark,
  Stronger it grew each hour,

Till the time for the waiting is past, soul,—
  Now thou shalt rise to thy power.

Far in the deep recesses of mind,
  Into thy spirit I come,
And my mantle around thee I'll fling, soul,
  Wrap thee, and make it thy home.

Doubt me no longer! Thou feelest now
  Strangely within thee rise
All the powers I have promised to thee, soul,
  Powers that exalt to the skies.

Rouse to the work that is waiting thee!
  Trust in the power divine!
And the spirit of song thou hast craved, soul,
  Thine, shall in fulness be thine.

POET.

I CAN no longer doubt, for in my heart
I feel a newer, richer life-blood start;
And all my soul is quivering with delight,
And glows like some new day just sprung from night.
My very brain seems quickened with a spell,
And floods of harmony within me swell,

As though some pitying angel's hand had rolled
The stone from sepulchre that held my soul—
Had troubled all the waves within me deep,
And waked long-silent voices from their sleep.
It is as though my heart sang, and each vein
Caught up the tone and rolled it on again;
As if each breath to each in rhyme was set,
And every thought its promised joy had met.
The wind is whispering through the forest trees,—
They answer, swaying to the passing breeze;
The rill that leaps and dances at my feet,
The music of the whispering winds repeats.
And every flower, with upturned, trusting eye,
That gazes toward the deep-blue summer sky,
And every hill and every mountain dell
Is wrapped and bathed in this mysterious spell.
And as I gaze, the sky that hangs above,
Droops over me with look of tender love,
As if 'twere mantle of the passing God,
That trailed toward earth to tell where He has trod.
Upon the whole with thrilling awe I look:
At last it stands revealed,—a Living Book
Unclasped, unsealed for me to read this hour,
And filled and glowing with intensest power.
'Tis one grand Poem: in my soul I see
Line after line unfold and speak to me,
Rich, full of gems of priceless power and thought;

Here is the treasure I so long have sought.
I've read earth's poets, thought by thought conned o'er,
Turned page on page of old, mysterious lore;
Bright gems I've found on many a brilliant page,
Of poets, teachers, written in their age;
But here I see the Mighty Thinker, here
Stands out the lesson of a higher sphere,
A living Poem written by God's hand,
And worthy of the Artist, solemn, grand,
And yet so sweet, the heart can dream of Heaven,
And of the Giver by what he has given.
I read this Poem; in its every line
Great Nature's truths in starry beauty shine;
And solemn grandeur never felt before
Steals through my soul—I worship, I adore!
An hour ago I thought it but the earth,—
Few joys for me, and they of little worth,—
But now it spreads, a type of that bright home
Beyond the misty darkness of the tomb.
It opens like a scroll to meet my view;
I see God's finger writing something new.
E'en as I gaze, still line on line is given,
Still pointing nearer to the gate of heaven.
Why, everything's a song, and sings its soul
In its true life; the parts but make the whole.
And oh, how poor are words! how more than weak!
Beside this work of God I cannot speak.

This mighty poem, in each different part,
Strikes home with awe sublime, and fills my heart,
Until each thought rolls back in its despair,
And dares not utter its weak idyl there;
So small, so slight, beside this word of God,
I bow in silent worship on the sod.
A half-hour since I felt such rising power,
It seemed my soul could spring to meet the hour,
And from its depths should rise one star of thought
To light my little life; yet, ere I caught
And held the power, and fashioned to my will,
To consciousness I woke with sudden thrill;
To know mysterious beauty round me spread,—
This God-like Poem,—and I bow my head,
A silent worshipper at this great shrine,
And feel as naught amid this work divine;
Hushed into silence by this mighty Word
That all the depths within me strangely stirred.
One gleam of sudden and of thrilling light
Swept o'er my soul amid its darkest night.
It cleared my vision, Nature's truth to see,
Unveiled its deep and hidden mystery;
It showed my utter nothingness to grasp
The mighty truths thy Spirit did unclasp.
It showed me small beside the Grand and Great,
Until I tremble at the open gate,
And dare not enter with unhallowed feet

The temple, where the Artist I may meet,
Who poured his Spirit into every line,
And left the impress of a soul divine.
What am I, God, that I should dare to speak
My poor, faint words in childish rhyme and weak,
Beside Thy anthem in its grandest roll,
Whose words are stars, the universe the whole?
I can but prostrate lie in silence deep,
Hushed, wrapped in awe, and closely round me keep
Earth's veil material, shading half my eye,
Lest, seeing more, I with thy greatness die.
With this one prayer: O Father, pity me!
I cannot check the wish to be like Thee!
Though crushed and humbled that I nothing stand,
Beside the work of thy eternal hand,
Still in this darkest night of my despair
To see the garb of littleness I bear,
Yet is there something deep within me, deep,
With all my strength I cannot hush to sleep.
It will keep crying through the weary night,
It will keep turning toward thy heavenly light,
It will lift up its forehead from the dust,
And seek audacious to behold the Just,
And pass beyond the temple-gate, and know,
And see the source from whence this Great could flow;
That will not turn away its restless eye,
But prays to see, if, seeing, it must die!

SPIRIT OF BEAUTY, *singing.*

WE rejoice! we rejoice! for the River of Life
Has been poured over thee, with its beauty all rife.
Thou hast caught but one glimpse of the soul of the sod,
And thy spirit hath bowed to its Spirit, its God.
Thou hast seen but one gleam of the Great and the
Grand,
But one volume that's writ by the mightiest Hand,
And thy soul has shrunk back at its greatness sublime,
And thou fearest to pass to that far purer clime.
It is well, it is well. Had it waked no new power,
Thou wouldst stand in thy strength and rejoice in this
hour;
But the light of the Greater has dawned in thy soul,
And its anthems drown thine in their mightier roll.
But rejoice, O thou dreamer! for thee there is hope;
With the great and the grand shall thy spirit yet cope;
For the weakness, the trembling, that comes to thee
now,
Shall yet stamp with God's signet thy thought-tortured
brow.
Thou hast bathed in the fountain,—'tis well, it is
well!
Thou shalt bathe yet again till a far brighter spell
Shall be woven around thee, and thou shalt be strong,—
This the proof that thy soul has not waited too long.

Genius.

Lie not so prostrate in the dust
  Because the God is great!
Or lose thy faith in inborn powers,
  Or tarry at the gate.
Thou sayest well; the power within
  Keeps crying every day,
To know God's truth, — and even God
  Will not be thrust away.

Because it is one tiny spark
  Of that Immortal Mind,
And like its Sire — the mighty God —
  No power can wholly bind.
Chain down thy thought — it breaks the chain —
  And crush it with strong hand,
It Sampson-like shall upward leap,
  And burst away its band.

Shalt thou turn hopeless from thy task,
  At what *His* hand has done,
E'en though, with all this mightiness,
  Thy God has just begun?
Thou art a creature of his hand,
  And wilt thou call it naught?
Thou art a part of His great plan —
  A strength should thus be taught.

Thou art a Poem in thyself,
One writing every day;
Line after line is every thought,
Ne'er to be swept away.
Thou art a part of that great whole —
The whole, so grand, sublime,
Without thee would be incomplete —
One necessary rhyme.

Then in this thought arise! be strong!
Though now it binds thy sight,
Soon thou shalt better read thyself
Within its purer light.
The very greatness shall awake
Somewhat more grand in thee,
Till strong and earnest in thy thought,
Thou shalt grasp hands — be free.

No matter, soul, how small a part
Thou findest here to fill,
Be up and ready for that work,
And do it with a will.
As grand as earth may lie outspread,
O'erarched by you blue sky,
As mighty as the planets pass,
And fill their place on high; —

Yet is thy soul — though small and weak —
  Far greater than them all,
For it can hear Jehovah speak,
  And list the angels' call.
And it can reason, think, and will,
  And leave its impress here,
And do the work the God has done,
  Though in a smaller sphere.

Man is the one Grand Poem, one, —
  The greatest God has given;
Its first low strains are sung on earth,
  'Tis finished but in heaven.
Then write thyself, thy living soul,
  In strong, deep words of love,
And cast the Godlike thought o'er earth,
  That thou hast caught above.

Pour out the fulness of thy soul
  In anthems strong and deep,
And other hearts shall catch them up,
  And all their sweetness keep.
'Twill be one voice among the rest.
  A diapason grand,
To sweep in one eternal tone,
  And echo through the land.

Take heart! Because the God is great,
  It should not make thee weak;
Thou art a part of that Great Power,
  Thy life of his must speak.
'Tis earnest of what thou shalt be,
  That thou art born of him;
Lift up thy forehead from the dust,
  And enter boldly in!

Thy smallest thought has something good,—
  It gives the mind a strength
By which it sends another forth,
  Which shall have power at length.
Press forward in the search for good,
  Press forward in the race,
And in God's beauty and his truth
  Thou'lt see him face to face!

Poet.

I WILL look up; though slight and small
Beside the God, yet I am all
His power has fashioned me to stand,—
I am the work of His great hand.
As such I must be worthy him,
Though poor and weak, though faint and dim
Beside the glory of his power;
Yet am I living in this hour

A tiny spark from that great Sun,
A life in littleness begun,
But still to grow and brighter stand,
As touched and fashioned by His hand.
All nature stretches grand and great,
To meet the sky in royal state;
Its varied beauties perfect shine,
Wrapped in a glory most divine.
I must be moulded with the rest,
In my own place as surely blest;
And I will stand upon this sod,
Yet lift my face to find the God.
I am thy child, O Artist grand!
One little stanza by thy hand,
Thine offspring; I've a claim on Thee,—
I know thou carest yet for me.
And Thou wilt give me strength and power,
And over me thy glory shower,
If I stand up all pure and free,
And like a child shall ask of Thee.

[*Prays.*

O Father! guard me with thy power—
  A spark struck from thy sun:—
Wilt give me strength to do my work,
  Somewhat as thou hast done?

O Father! claim and call thy child,
  And let me hear thy voice;
All reverent I ask of Thee,
  Beauty and power — my choice!

I feel thy great parental Love
  Flow deep through all my soul;
I hear the anthem of thy power
  In mighty cadence roll.

I feel Thy presence round me cast;
  It binds me with a spell;
My soul is closer drawn to thine, —
  O Father! it is well.

I hear Thy hushed, mysterious tread
  Through sky, and air, and sod;
Thy mantle wraps and folds thy child,
  Father and Giver, — God!

Angels singing in the distance — Voices drawing nearer.

Child of earth! how sweet the music
  Of an asking, waiting soul!
To the inner courts of heaven
  Do its richest anthems roll.

We have watched and waited for thee, —
  Waited through the weary hours:

Thou hast risen into beauty ;
  In it thou shalt find thy powers.

Thou hast felt the mighty presence
  Of the God, within thy mind ;
There's the only living fountain,
  Only there great wealth we find.

It has brought thy soul toward heaven :
  Thou has met us in the skies,
As we came to meet, to greet thee,
  Came to bless thy waiting eyes.

Poesy has cast her mantle,
  Beauty bathed thee with her spell,
Genius lit the fires within thee,
  And thy soul leaps up, — 'tis well !

We will shed a richer fragrance ;
  Tones forgotten on the earth,
Through thy lips shall come to mortals —
  Springing once again to birth.

Thou shalt stand like ancient priestess
  In the temples long ago ;
From thy lips strange words prophetic
  Half unconsciously shall flow.

Thou shalt be a link uniting
  Worlds that seeemed so far away,
Thou shalt be like beam of morning,
  Ushering a golden day.

Keep God's mantle close around thee,
  Lest the world shall stain thy soul,
And the rich strings lose the beauty
  Of their anthem's deepest roll.

Stand above sin's dark pollution,
  Keep thy soul all pure and white,
Clear, transparent, where may enter
  Floods of glory and of light.

Walk amid the dark and lowly, —
  If it needs be, vice and sin, —
With the voice that we shall give thee,
  From their haunts, God's souls to win:

But above it, still above it
  Hold thy spirit evermore, —
In the world, and yet not of it,
  Pointing to a viewless shore.

Keep thy spirit still majestic,
  As the angels glorious stand,

And archangel's power shall reach thee,—
Lead and guide thee by the hand.

Keep the beauty of thy spirit,
And we'll pour our wealth o'er thee,
Till thy presence brings a blessing;
In it souls shall spring forth free.

Thou shalt be thyself a Poem,
All thy life an anthem grand,
Rising, swelling, upward sweeping,
Its last strain in spirit land.

Child of earth! we stoop to bless thee,
Take the power we gladly give!
Beauty, genius, strength be with thee,
Grandly wear them, grandly live!

Friends who've left the shores of earth-life,
Havened on the other side,
With their living presence guard thee,
With their tender love shall guide.

Clasp the hands now stretched to meet thee,
Till they lead to our blest shore,
And the angels joy to greet thee,
Entering at the golden door!

POET.

MY God! what vision fills my soul!
I seem to near my wished-for goal.
How have I yearned to hear some tone
Of those I loved and called my own,
Passed strangely to the other shore,
Haunting my spirit evermore!

And did I hear the angels sing,
Whose echoes through my spirit ring?
And shall I have that promised power?
O God! I bless thee for this hour!
And all my soul floats out in song,
I've watched and waited, prayed so long;

Yet dared not hope this bliss would come,—
That beings from that Brighter Home
Would give me power to see and know,
And thrill my spirit with this glow
Of living light and fire divine:
O Father, all my soul is thine!

SPIRIT OF POESY.

TAKE this harp! and let thy spirit
  Touch its chords with thrilling strain;
Let thy richest thoughts ensphere it,
  Till they answer back again.

Wait not, thinking, still divining
What the song that thou shalt sing!
Pour the wealth thy soul enshrining,
Trembling over every string!

POET.

THE words of song come floating to my lips,
Like perfume on the wind;
Aye, thought keeps struggling into rhythmic words—
Long pent within my mind,—

As though my soul would tremble forth in song,
In freedom's ecstasy;
And lift itself with one great sunward flight,
And lose itself in Thee.

Fountain of light, of truth, and perfect love!
My soul leaps forth to try,
Upon the wings of Song, to reach thy home,
Or in its efforts die!

[*Improvises.*

I spurn my prison-house of earth,—
The *body* where I've lain
Like captive in his cold, damp cell,
Thrice-bound with heavy chain.

The grated bars that hid my view,
  And shut me dark within,
The massive door, the heavy bolt,
  Shall never bind again.

One breath of freedom and of strength
  Has never come to me;
But now a hand has loosed the bars,
  And I will step forth free.
I gaze upon truth's sunny sky,
  I list the song of love,
And Beauty with her starry eyes
  Bends o'er me from above.

And oh! within myself I feel
  A burning power to know,
Beyond the prison-gates to pass,
  Let watch and warder go;
And leave behind me every power
  That dared my soul to bind,
And follow after my desire
  That's fleeter than the wind,—

Beyond the earth, beyond the glow
  Of sunshine on the stream,
Beyond the visions of my youth,
  Beyond each fairy dream;

And never tire and never wait,
  Until the thirst within,
Is slaked at some bright fountain far
  From earth's tumultuous din.

Oh, how like falcon from his gyves,
  On hunter's hand set free,
My lightning thought takes sudden flight,
  And whistles back for me!
Speed on, speed on, O eagle-eyed,
  And find the gates of heaven!
Speed on! and never leave that gate,
  Till God's rich truths are given.

Cling closely when the angels pass,
  Till they shall take thee in,
And wash thy garments pure and white,
  To stain no more with sin!
On, on! like deer that hears the sound
  Of hunters on his track;
And if thou findest thy true home,
  No power shall send thee back!

[*The harp falls from her hands, while her eager face, upturned eyes, her outstretched arms and whole attitude reveal the soul just ready to leap its barriers and follow the song.*

GENIUS.

CALL back thy thoughts, nor let them burst away
In such delight toward regions of bright day!
'Tis well to form thy soul's deep wealth in song,
But not alone to airy flights belong
The Poet's gifts! 'Tis beautiful to feel
The fountain leap within the soul,—its seal
All broken,—while the living waters free
Toss out their spray toward eternity.
There's such a rush and tide of burning thought,
As if an angel's fire the soul had caught;
There's such a luxury in the rising power,
I marvel not it bears thee in this hour,
Like some white bark amid the tossing night,
On through the breakers, toward the beacon light.
Yet not for that alone we give thee power,
But for still greater use has come this dower.
The Poet's mission is to deeply think:
Not always should he rise, but he must sink
His soul unto the level of each thought;—
From every phase of life his power is caught.
Like Franklin, he may fly his kite toward heaven,
And catch the lightning when the clouds are riven;
But yet, like Fulton, he must bring this power
To each day's use, fit for each passing hour;
And then, like Morse, must send it on its track,
Till thought to thought in souls shall answer back.

The poet has been called a dreamer vain,
Who idly sings his still more idle strain,
To please the ear and fancy's careless eye,
To catch imagination passing by;
A thing of beauty, like the summer flower,—
To live, to bloom, to perish in an hour.
But 'tis not so. The Poet of the soul,
Whose thrilling tones in strange, deep music roll,
Who sends the lightning of his thought to men,
Shall bring a burning answer back again.

The world's true Poet teaches common things,
And makes a living power of what he sings;
Catches the Real for his corner-stone,
And builds his pyramid, with power unknown,
Of real life, of real burning tears,
Of real soul-deep grief, and real fears,
Of heroes living in the present day,
As well as heroes, martyrs, passed away,
Of true devotion in the lowly heart;—
And every passion still must bear its part;—
Of love requited, and of love misplaced,
That leaves a mark no outward eye has traced.
True moral worth must be the crowning head,
True spiritual beauty the bright halo shed;
The soul's ideal stand the arch above—
The rainbow, bending o'er it all in love,

Mingling the whole; the base (the granite rock
Of real strength and power to bear the shock)
Of common facts and common thoughts of men, —
The heart's deep passions glowing out again;
The soul's Ideal looming in the skies,
Toward which man turns his weary, aching eyes,
Until it grows the real of his life,
And smoothes his path, and hushes all his strife.
It is the Poet's mission to descend,
And all the influence of his spirit lend
To those who still pursue the beaten way,
And think of nought beyond the present day;
And scatter flowers, and rainbow tints, and song,
To mingle with the dull, material throng,
Until they learn to love, and to aspire,
And reach for beauty, till it draws them higher.

The Poet is the prophet, if he's true;
He grasps the past, and points unto the new;
He links the ages, like the angel's hand,
Who stands, "one foot on sea and one on land";
Sings of what is, and then of what must be,
When man from all that's gross arises free;
Points with an eye of hope and hand of power
Unto a brighter, better, coming hour;
With heart of fire and tongue of living flame,
Withers the thought that ever stoops to shame,

And makes each soul its own true birthright see,
And rise from what it is, more pure to be.
The Poet is the priest, to walk the sod,
And stand the type, the image of the God:
In noble word, in noble deed sublime
To live, and send his power to future time;
To speak such words as seize upon the heart,
And, half unconsciously, a nobler part
Help it perform; and thrill the listening mind
Until no chain that spirit's strength can bind.
Until each latent power shall upward leap
From out its long, mysterious, dreamless sleep,
Quick-started into life by sudden thrill,
And nevermore to sleep, but to fulfil
Its higher work, its destiny on earth,—
To make still other souls of purer worth.
Else is he no true Poet; though he sings,
And airy fancy round him closely clings,
And rainbow mantles wrap him in their light,
And morning's glories gather fair and bright;
He's but a mid-day meteor in the sky,—
An hour shall pass and all his light shall die.
But he that burns and beams with steady blaze,
Like some fair planet in its heavenly rays,—
Mild but intense, that lights the blue of heaven,
And has eternal life unto it given,—
'Tis he that lights the wandering, darkened race,

And sees God's beauties ever face to face.
He's the *true* Poet, who shall daily bring
To man this rich and soul-deep offering;—
The knowledge of himself, his inborn power,
The use, the beauty of each present hour,
The hidden meaning of great Nature's laws,
The cure of sin, as well as show its cause.
He is the Teacher who shall point man's way
Unto a brighter and a better day,
With winning words of beauty and of love,
Calling his soul for evermore above;
Still making purer with each thought he speaks,
Still urging higher as he onward seeks,
Refining still each thought, until his soul
Shall rise where it can grasp and see the whole;
Making the common mind press forward still,
Until with grander thoughts each chord shall thrill,
And power shall wake to lead him toward the skies,
And he becomes the strong, the good, the wise.
The Poet is the Thinker; he must trace
Through nature up to see the Father's face.

It is no light, no common thing to wear
The mantle of true Poesy, and share
The brightness of her triple crown of light,—
Power, Purity, and Beauty,—these her might.
It is a solemn thing to reach thy hand

To grasp her treasure, and to seek to stand
Upon the hallowed ground where mingles three
Such potent spells; — now must thou worthy be.
Be but the REAL POET! be the true!
While bright around thy path our gifts we strew;
Or let thy harp forever mouldering lie,
Never again its thrilling strings to try.
Attempt the best! Though failing in thy part,
Still thou shalt reach some sorrow-stricken heart.
Attempt the high, the pure, the true, the great,
Though at the portals long thy soul must wait!
Catch rich, grand thoughts from fountains pure
above,
Then pour them out with thine own thoughts in love!
Mark every place with flowers where thou hast trod,
And let thy path lead always toward thy God!
Then, though thy strains are faint, and low, and
weak,
Something of beauty must within them speak;
Something of greatness, truth, within them shine,
Sooner or late to tell their source divine!
Ah, let thy harp ring forth with burning song,
Until it shames from every heart the wrong;
And bid its richest music thrill the soul,
Till, echoing back, responsive notes shall roll!
Thou singest not to soar beyond the skies,
But 'tis to hush poor Sorrow's wailing sighs;

Aye, not to pass beyond the gate of heaven,
But that some light to others may be given.
Thou singest not to burst from earth all free,
But to teach others how to sing like thee;
And sweeter, better, stronger than thine own,
To pour o'er other hearts their thrilling tone.
This thy reward, — not perfect freedom given, —
To know thou leadest others nearer Heaven!

POET.

I WILL be strong. These words of truth I'll keep
Treasured within my spirit's chambers deep.
And I will only turn my watching eyes,
And send my thoughts afar beyond the skies,
To catch rich treasures from the bright above,
To pour o'er others, in their earnest love.
I'll only pass into the realms of Light,
To make more clear my own imperfect sight,
And catch the truths of heaven, the thoughts that burn,
For which I know each soul like mine must yearn.
These will I mingle with the things of life,
To cast a halo o'er its pain and strife,
And give a Beauty to the tasks of men,
Until the weary shall take heart again.
I'll be content, though never strong and great
As I have wished, though lingering at the gate;

I'll think my own best thought and give it word.
Content if but *some* hearts are strangely stirred,
And feel new powers awake their depths within,
That rise and work, and stand above all sin.
I'll be the Worker, not the dreamer here;
Or only dream of some far brighter sphere,
Because I know that dream is good and true,
And real, though to others strange and new.
I'll cherish still ideals great and grand,
Before me like the pyramids to stand;
So shall they lure and beckon me still higher,
And they shall call from far, and say, "Aspire!"
For though *ideals* in the present day,
They shall be *reals* yet, and bear the sway.
I'll dream, and work, and think, all as in one,
Then, only then, my mission is begun.—
Oh, all ye Powers that strengthen and make bright,
Do ye assist me from this wond'rous night!
Angels that live where mortals have not trod!
Helper of all! my life's great giver — God!

Fairies of the Greenwood.

We have heard thy prayer,
And we bring the fair
  From flowery cup and bell;
And the greenwood tree,
From its leaves to thee,
  Shall whisper a fairy spell.

The mosses so green
In their silver sheen,
  Shall send thee the spirit of rest;
And the violet's eye,
As it looks to the sky,
  Shall speak to thy soul of the blest.

And the Druid oak
Hath its oracle spoke,
  It beareth a strength to thee;
For its stalwart limb,
And its trunk so grim,
  Are the symbols of the free;—

While the clinging vine,
That will always twine,
  As it climbs to reach the sky,
Closely round its form,
Through the sun or storm,
  And with it would gladly die,—

Is a type of the Love
That shall rise above
  All selfishness here below;
Unasked it is given,—
Like a breeze out of heaven,
  Uncaring, unthinking, will flow.

The sunshine and shade
Through the forest laid,
  On its carpet of green so bright,
Is the type of this life,
Of its bliss and its strife,
  Grief's darkness, and joy's pure light.

And the wind that sweeps
Through the forest deeps,
  Till the green leaves tremble within,
Is the type of pure thought
That is poured unsought,
  And saves and cleanses from sin.

And the anthem grand,
When the mighty hand
  Of the tempest is on the oak,
Is the voice of Him —
When the day was dim —
  That "Light" for Creation spoke.

Oh, under the tree
There is wealth for thee!
  Far in the dim wood-shade,
Where no foot has trod,
Are the truths of God —
  We will show thee where they're laid.

Then come to our nooks!
They are living books,
  Where the soul may gaze and read;
And treasure it well,
There's a hidden spell
  To hearts that will take good heed.

And seek us for aye!
Through the summer day,
  Thou shalt often hear our tone;
We'll reveal to thee,
'Neath the greenwood tree,
  Our truths until then unknown.

Kind Nature shall teach
What no lips can preach,—
  Shall teach on her own green sod,
Thrilling truths to man,
Of the laws and plan
  Of her own — Great Nature's God!

Then come where we dwell!
We will weave a spell
  That shall burn through the songs you sing;
Keep close to the sod,
Yet looking to God,
  And our mantle around thee shall cling!

Naiads of the Fountain.

I.

We will throw the spray from our laughing rills,
As they leap and dance from the summer hills.
There shall be a song in the brooklet's flow,
If thine ear is close, it will let thee know;
Aye, something of beauty, whispering still,
That the heart of youth and of age shall thrill.

II.

In the mountain spring there shall be a thought,
That in vain, perhaps, through the years you've sought.
From the brook that flows to the river grand,
We will sometimes lift it — our magic wand, —
And a beauty send to thy spirit's deep,
That shall wake some thought from its midnight sleep.

III.

Thou shalt hear us best when thou art alone; —
Though unseen by others, to thee well known.
In the little lakes, in the mountain dell,
There shall lie all mirrored our magic shell;
Thou hast but to look, and our best truths see,
And the things of God be made known to thee.

IV.

Thou must never think that the waters lie,
With no truth to speak in their murmured sigh.
There are spells of beauty on every sod,
There are fruits that speak of the maker, God;
But the founts are clear, and they show a trace
In their clear, bright depths of His very face.

V.

By the rill's pure bed let thy coming feet,
All the sprites that live in their depths oft greet.
By the mountain spring let thy steps still stray,
And be wandering oft to earth's founts away;
And a charm shall come to thy voice and word,
That has never before from thy lips been heard.

VI.

In their mirrors bright thou shalt see thy face,
And shall learn to add still a newer grace.
In the pure, rich thought that shall come to thee,
In the light that makes all thy spirit free,
Thou shalt learn to weep nevermore, nor pine,
For our founts shall leap, and the spray be thine!

Spirits of the Air.

Yes, we hasten to answer thee, hasten to come
From our palace of splendor, the sun-lighted dome!
We have treasures of beauty, so bright and so fair,
Oh, we would that more mortals were willing to share!
We have brought the sun's rays — they shall make thee a pen
That shall tip as with fire all thy words unto men;
And we'll bring thee for paper, on which thou shalt write
All thy songs of pure joy, and thy visions of night,
E'en the clouds in our heaven, in their lights and their shade,
With the gleams of pale sunshine that over them strayed.
When thou writest of sin, we will bring thee the cloud
That is dark with the tempest,— the storm's blackened shroud;
When thou writest of joy, we will give thee the gold-
Tinted clouds, with a sunbeam in every fold.
When thou singest of hope, "silver linings" we'll bring,
Till far brighter and sweeter the songs thou shalt sing.
When thou speakest of woe, and of carnage and blood,
We will bring thee the clouds where the sun has just stood,
Gleaming gorgeous with crimson, — the hour ere he set, —

Where it seems in his passing some dark foe he met,
Till they grappled in frenzied and deadly embrace,
And this deluge of blood had enveloped his face,
And he lay on his bier in his gorgeous array,
With his clouds that trailed crimson while passing away.
We will bring thee the blue from the deep, summer sky,
On thy breast as an ægis protecting to lie;
We will bring thee the winds that sweep strong through the heaven,
With the hurricane's voice, as in thunder 'tis given;
And the whirlwinds that pass in their storm-bannered car,
For a moment so near us, then travelling far.
And all these thou shalt have when strong powers thou wouldst wake,
When the tyrant should tremble and shivering quake,
When the patriot's harp should leap up with one gush
Of true love for his country, then onward would rush,
Like the hurricane's sweep, till he falls on his foe,
Like the whirlwind, to scatter, like that to bring woe.
We will send a sweet breeze when thou speakest of love,
That will woo and will beckon the spirit above.
We will give thee soft zephyrs to breathe with a sigh,
Of the captive's damp cell and the tear-stricken eye,
We will send thee the winds of the autumn to wail,

Aye, the moaning, the sighing, the murmuring gale,
When lie cold the brave forms on the far battle-plain,
And the orphans and widows weep wild o'er the slain.
But if thus they have died in defence of the Right,
Not sad dirges alone, not the shadows of night,
Will we bring thee to shed where their silent forms
are,
But the glory and light of our own morning star.
In the hour thou wouldst write of a soul that has
sprung
From some error or stain that around it has clung,
Or some mind that was tempted almost to its fall,
Yet arose in its strength still triumphant o'er all.;
Of great deeds in their splendor, of good they have
brought,
Of the light and the glory the strong mind has caught,
Of a nation that wrestled with sin and with wrong,
That arose from the conflict, triumphant and strong,
We will send the grand anthems that sweep through
the sky,
Eternal, unceasing, that never can die.
And when thou wouldst speak of the soul that has past
Through the portals of death, and its dark mantle cast,
Yet immortal shall live on some far brighter shore,
To rejoice in pure bliss, evermore, evermore,
We will bear the bright rainbow to glow through thy
speech,

With the power of its beauty life's promise to teach;
For its grand arch triumphal shall rise o'er it all,
And disperse the dark clouds that hang round like a pall.
We will snatch the bright stars from their place in the heaven,
All their brightness and truth to the world shall be given;
And the lights streaming up through the north in their fire,
We will send thee, to teach every soul to aspire,
Till they quiver and burn through thy songs as the sky,
And they bear on their wings every spirit on high.
We will pour out our gifts. If thou turnest to see
And know of our glories, we'll give them to thee.

Genii of the Ocean.

We have heard in our depths profound,
From thy lips a murmuring sound,
And we thought it breathed a prayer;
And that spirits of the air,
And the naiads bright and fair,
Had taken thee to their care,
And were weaving spells for thee,
Underneath the greenwood tree,
In the fountains, on the lea,

In the fair blue sky we see,
Till the voice came down, and we
Have arisen from our deep,
Where our royal court we keep,
Where the brave young sailors sleep,
Where the mermaids o'er them weep,
And the sea-weeds round them creep,—
Yes, to bring each bidden spell,
From the caves wherein we dwell,
And to let our own tones swell,
With a sound like,—"It is well!"

We have brought the pearl from its ocean-bed,
All its soft, pale light o'er thy words to shed,
And the shells with delicate rainbow hue,
For their wondrous tints o'er thy work we'd strew,
Till they teach the light and the power of God,
Where the foot of mortal has never trod,
Far away, away, from the dark green sod.

And we've brought the coral shining,
And the sea-weed ever twining,
And a thousand nameless things,
That around our portal clings;
Gems and jewels from our caves,
Spray and foam from out the waves,
And the treasures of the world,

Into our deep caverns hurled,
Ere the light was wide unfurled,
  To bless the earth in love;
Just to teach what unseen worth
In all unknown deeps has birth,
Hidden from the outer earth,
  Never brought above,
Till some kindly hand has lent
All its energies, and sent
Some one on this mission bent,
  To find the treasure deep;
Some skilful diver of the soul,
Who dares the waves that round him roll,
To find each part and learn the whole,
  As treasured store to keep.

For within the human mind
Such deep treasures thou wilt find,
  Though the form seems rude;
Underneath some frowning mask,
If thy soul knows how to ask,
  Thou mayst find a good.

Search the sea of thought forever,
Be its own true, earnest diver,
And to earth thou'lt be a giver
  Of rich gems of light.

Search the deep, mysterious things,
Cast the mantle back that clings,
And to earth at last it brings
  Powers that chase the night.

We are Genii of the Sea,
We will always answer thee,
  When thou callest for our aid;
But search deeply and search well,
Till thou findst the hidden spell,
  Moving more than we have said.

Under every ocean wave
There is still a hidden cave,
  With its pearl and shell;
Deep in every human soul
There are powers that ever roll,
  Each a potent spell.

Hast thou not heard our waves' great song,
Their strange, deep voices murmuring long,—
  Hast thou not heard our tone?
We're ever singing some wild strain,
That comes and goes, then comes again,
  To many hearts unknown.

Oh, list the Ocean's mighty voice!
The deepest anthems are its choice,—
  And ever hear them roll;
And catch the strain and let it ring,
Until its own deep song you sing
  Through every listening soul.

One poem grand is this our strain,
Repeated o'er and o'er again,
  Yet ever just as new;
Catch up the thought, and let it sweep
Through every listening spirit's deep,
  Until they learn it true.

There's inspiration in the tone,
There's knowledge of the great Unknown,
  To fill thy mind with awe;
There shalt thou see His mighty power,
There listen in each passing hour,
  And read his written law.

In thoughtful hours, come read this page,
Rewritten through each age on age,
  And learn its living lore;
And hear the wild waves dash and beat,
And strive to firmly plant their feet,
  Upon the treach'rous shore.

And teach men 'tis not all in vain,
Not fruitless effort, fruitless pain,
  It keeps its native strength;
And through this action, through this strife,
Calls forth its latent power, its life,
  And grows more pure at length.

Teach this to man, and let him see
Such should his life forever be,
  And he should purer grow;
And in his efforts and his pain,
Though seeming fruitless, seeming vain,
  He'll learn God's truth to know.

Go stand "beside the sea-beat shore,
And turn its pebbles o'er and o'er,
  And listen to its sigh;"
Thine every line shall catch a tone
That will become thy very own,
  In thy soul's chambers lie, —

Until that soul is full of spells,
And pearls and corals and of shells,
  More bright than of the sea;
The shells, the pearls, the gems of thought,
That long so vainly thou hast sought,
  Shall live all bright in thee.

Come listen oft, and thou shalt hear
The voices from the other sphere,
  Where mortal has not trod;
And thou shalt write thy burning word,
Until each human heart is stirred,
  And turns to know of God.

GODDESS OF THE SOUL.

MY home is in the human mind,
  I read its inmost thought,
And I have heard thy earnest prayer; —
  I bring thee what is sought.
The greenwood deep will give thee power,
  The fountains in their play,
The treasures of the sky enrich,
  Deep caverns far away.

But still there needs a greater power,
  To speak to soul — to mind,
And only in its hidden depths,
  That power may any find.
All Nature helps thee in thy work,
  Go read her open book,
Thou canst not con its page too much,
  'Twill pay thy earnest look;

But search the deepest human soul,
  And know its wants, its need,
And in its hidden caves of thought
  Its every feeling read.
'Tis only then that thou canst speak
  Unto the deep within,
And rouse it to a higher life,
  And save it from its sin.

'Tis when thy fingers know its chords,
  That thou canst touch it well,
And weave thy thoughts in gushing song,
  To bind it with a spell.
'Tis when thy ear can listen deep
  To voices in the soul,
And hear the dirges weep and wail,
  And mark the anthems roll;

And hear the anguished cry for light,
  Amid the darkest hour,
That thou canst answer to its prayer,
  And touch it in its power.—
I'll bear to thee from human souls,
  Through telegraphic wires
So fine no mortal eye can see,
  Its wishes, its desires.

I'll bear the strength of other minds
  To mingle with thine own,
To swell thy song to wilder force,
  And give it deeper tone.
I'll snatch the fire in burning hearts,
  And scatter it o'er thine,
I'll catch the spirit from true souls,
  To make still more divine.

I'll link thy soul with mystic bands
  By strange and unseen law,
Until a strength, a hidden power,
  From others thou shalt draw.
And thou wilt give it back again
  In rich and thrilling song,
In words that still uphold the right,
  And trample down the wrong.

Thou art to be the people's voice,
  To speak their own best thought,
For which they could not find the words,
  Though long in vain they sought.
The People's poet thou shalt be —
  Interpreter of truth,
Speaking all hopeful unto age,
  And strengthening unto youth.

Turn often to thy soul's deep shrine,
  Its sacred fane within,
And leave far back, aye, very far,
  The world's dark strife and din.
And worship at this inner shrine,
  And earnest call for me,
And I will bring my holiest gifts,
  And pour them out to thee!

Poet.

Oh, voice on voice, and Power on Power,
Seem watching, helping me this hour!
I am not worthy this to share,
And oh, how can I think to wear
The mantles that they cast o'er me,
And hope to keep unstained and free!
Yet, Spirits of the earth and air,
And ocean wave and fountain fair,
And Goddess of the human soul,
That points to my long-wished-for goal,
Angels that bend from brighter skies,
In whose sweet faces, loving eyes,
I see the friends long passed away
Unto the bright and golden day,
Father of Love, who watcheth me,
Help me to be all worthy Thee!

FAIRIES, NAIADS, SPIRITS, AND GENII.

WE help thee, we've tried thee,
We guard thee, we guide thee,
No ill shall betide thee,
For we are beside thee,
  To help evermore!

[*Echo*, Evermore!

Our Spirits shall bless thee,
Our love shall caress thee,
Our gifts shall impress thee,
Still drawing thy spirit
To yet truer merit,
The life to inherit,
Where thy friends shall all meet thee,
Where the loved ones shall greet thee,
And where naught shall defeat thee,
  On that blessed shore;
Where earth's heavy pain
That o'er thee has lain,
Shall come not again
  Nevermore, nevermore!

[*Echo*, Never — more!

FAIRIES, NAIADS, ETC.

Nevermore, nevermore!

[*Echo*, Nev — er — more!

SCENE II.

Evening. A lighted parlor. The members of the family, also a lady friend, seated at their separate employments. The father throws down the evening's paper, and turns to his daughter.

MR. SEYMOUR.

WHAT keeps thee, Ida, poring o'er that book?
I scarce have caught a single welcome look.
Had I not found my slippers waiting there,
All warm and nice beside my easy chair,
I should have doubted if thou wert at home —
Come, tell me what thou'rt reading, daughter, come!

[*She lays down her book, seats herself on his lap, and lays her head affectionately upon his shoulders.*

Ah, not too old to be my little pet!
I know thou art a woman — yes, and yet
It hardly seems a day has passed since thou
Wert but a little babe, a child, and now
I fear some gay young knight will win thy heart,
And leave for me not even one small part.
How is it, — shall I lose my summer flower?
It would, indeed, be but a mournful hour.

[*Pats her cheek.*

IDA, *playfully.*

Oh, never fear, I know there could not be
A man in all the world so kind to me,
As thou, my father, and I mean to stay
As long as hearts would miss me if away.

MR. SEYMOUR.

Well, well, no more; thy mother's half in tears
I do believe, at just these playful fears.
But, stay! thou hast not told me yet what page
Has held thee bound as silent as a sage.
I know thou art a book-worm, but to-night
I almost thought thy mind had taken flight.

IDA.

The book indeed is wonderful. Each line
With strange, rich gems of thought and beauty shines.
I wonder where the poet found the power
O'er every page such wealth of soul to shower.
It seems as though the pen was tipped with fire,
To touch the soul, and teach it to aspire.
Not lofty, far above the common mind,
But where each heart its own desire can find
Rewritten, and its answer strangely given,
Till led unconsciously on toward its heaven.
There is an earnestness in each new thought,

Some holy purpose every line has caught;
I can not tell the beauties that I see,
But it has woke new powers and thoughts in me.
It seems as though I could not sink again
To common thoughts and common cares and pain.
If I could keep the spirit of the page,
There'd come to *me* at least the Golden Age.
It does not give the author's real name,
I find no clue to tell from whence it came.
Its title, "The True Life:"—'tis given well!
And binds me strangely with an unseen spell.

MR. SEYMOUR.

And yet, a book that leads the mind away
From real life, and cares of every day,
With airy flights of fancy soaring high,
That leaves the listener floating in the sky,
Is not the power to make thee firm and strong
To meet the cares that unto life belong.
We find it not on any written page;—
My daughter, we must *make* the Golden Age!

IDA.

I did not mean it took my thoughts from earth;
It waked within me those of greater worth.
It made the tasks of life seem like a joy,
Its cares, its ills, too trifling to annoy;

And shed a calm and softened light o'er life,
That strangely swept away its cares and strife.
I say again, if I could keep the power
I've caught from that true Poet in this hour,
The world would be all beauty ; for the hand
Of some great earnest work would ever stand
Revealed to me, and in my life's true light
I'd still work on, because it leads to Right.

MR. SEYMOUR.

Then was it good. I love to hear thy voice
Speak words like these—it makes my heart rejoice.
I would not have thee throw thy life away
In careless ease, and childish, petty play :
I've prayed, a true and earnest life for thee,—
To see thee live it, will be heaven to me.

[*Loses himself in thought.*

I'll read the book—I like an earnest thought.
There's much that's trash, much better if unbought.
Hast read this book, Kate Walters ?

KATE.

No, not I!

For me 'tis much too prosy, and too dry.
I beg thy daughter's pardon, but I heard
Her read some parts, yet did not hear a word
That's in my style. I like Byronic verse,

Not Pope's nor Cowper's ; — this is even worse,
Forever bringing down to real life ; —
I'd rather burst away from all its strife,
And plunge into some deeply thrilling book,
Like Byron's "Corsair," or Moore's "Lalla Rookh."
And then with strange, new notions it is filled.
Let parsons preach, I say, what God has willed,
But this points out to life such lofty use,
Rather than try to live, I'd beg a truce.
'Tis my belief that when a person dies,
'Tis time enough to pass into the skies ;
That life on earth is given to enjoy
What good there is, ere it has time to cloy.
And then I think the heroine takes a stand
In that position God assigned to man.
I don't believe in "Woman's Rights ;" such stuff
I dread ; I'm sure that I have rights enough !

MR. SEYMOUR, *laughing*.

No one doubts that, as on some future day
Some luckless wight may have good cause to say !

KATE.

Well, have thy joke ! I've my opinion still.
I have no doubt thy daughter will fulfil
A higher life than mine, that runs to waste ;
I say, "God speed !" but I've a different taste.

MRS. SEYMOUR.

Why, Kate, I really thought thou hadst a heart,
That, when once touched, would see a better part.
Reared in such luxury, thou canst not know,
From what or whom thy countless blessings flow;
But with thy love of ease and happiness,
Thou hast not found the greatest charm to bless.
Joy lies not in the getting, that's not bliss;
This is the secret test, — thou'lt find it this:
Give, give, forget thyself, and always give!"
Thus find God's blessing, thus in pleasure live.

KATE.

It may be; but I think I'd rather get.
And, with thy own belief, should I regret.
I make the *giver* happier that he
Finds God's rich blessing when he gives to me?
A true philanthropist in my own way; —
Who'll dare dispute it, Mr. Seymour, say?

MR. SEYMOUR, (*smiling.*)

A sophist rather! but we can't expect
An heiress, belle, young Clifton's bride elect,
To look on life with unveiled, earnest eyes,
Or stop to weep where human suffering lies.
I well remember in my youthful day —
I half forget my hair is turning gray —

How thoughtless unto mirth I gave my heart,
Until keen anguish pierced it with her dart,
And woke me sudden to the sense of pain
In other hearts ; — it never slept again.
A child of fortune, like thyself, I clung
To pleasure, till my father's death-knell rung.
He died insolvent. O'er his honored name
The cold world hung the blackened pall of shame,
And called him base. It broke my mother's heart,
And I was left alone to bear my part,
With such a sudden sense of life's first pain,
As when once borne, can never come again.
I sank at first beneath the dreadful blow,
But soon I felt a deeper life-blood flow,
And all my soul rose up. That point began
My real life. Grief stamped me first a man.
I firmly breasted life's impetuous stream ;
I have succeeded far beyond my dream.
Wealth, fame and honor, now the world calls mine,
Two jewels for my heart forever shine ;
And in the love that gathers round my hearth,
I might forget the misery of earth,
But for this first great blow ; now my great prayer
Is that my bliss each human heart may share.
And if a day has passed, no act of mine
Has given joy for which the thousands pine,
I count it lost ; and with me, heart and hands,

I need not say that Mrs. Seymour stands.
Thou knowest her well ; the poor know better far;—
I need not tell thee what her merits are.
And this, my daughter, round whose life my heart
Clings with a love in which self bears no part,—
The only pledge of our long, mutual love,—
More than all else I've striven, far above
All thoughtlessness to elevate her mind,
The loftier beauty in this life to find,
That women often loses reared in wealth.
And, blessed with beauty, grace, and joys of health,
I could not bear to see her spend her youth,
Careless and vain, coquettish, proud, in truth
Like thousands whom indulgent parents rear,
So all unfitted for a woman's sphere,—
Just pretty women, fit to while away
Man's leisure hours some quiet summer day;
With winning smiles, and doll-like, quiet face,
And genteel small talk done with artist's grace;
With thoughts, opinions, aspirations tame,
And not one thought of life's true end and aim.
It pains my heart to see these fragile flowers
Step forth in life without a woman's powers,
And yet assume a woman's duties, state,
And failing, meet a sad and early fate.
It grieves me much—I speak it as a friend—
To see one blest as thou, thy best powers spend

In what seems so unworthy, trifling, vain;
And yet I would not give thy heart a pain.
But sometimes when I see thee move in light,
Amid the crowds in pleasure's halls at night,
And think such bliss is all in all to thee,
Thou canst not guess the pang that comes to me.
I loved thy father, and I love his child,—
Though far too wayward, and albeit too wild,—
And I can see beyond this brilliant haze,
To real life, and earnest future days,
When woman's duties come, sweet, but yet stern,
And call to thee from thoughtless scenes to turn,
And lay thy soul's best offering at a shrine
Where thou must mould still other minds by thine.
And if unequal to the task that's given,
How will thy heart with many a pang be riven,
And joys that seem so full of beauty now,
Will turn to dust and ashes on thy brow.
I would not have thee less the glad and gay,
I love thy leaping sunshine every day,
The waves of joy that sweep across thy soul;
I only wish, beneath their dash and roll
The germs of earnest purpose hidden slept,
And nobler, loftier thoughts their vigils kept,
To leap like Genii from the ocean cave,
Should storm and tempest come thy bark to save.
Forgive me, that I've spoken words so plain,

Perchance sometime they'll come to thee again.
Who knows? You smile; but words unheeded now,
May echo back in after days, and thou
Wilt give them audience, with better grace
Than I expect to win from that young face.

KATE.

I feel thy words, their truth and earnest love.
Thou knowest I have no friends I prize above
Thyself and thine; if aught could tame my heart,
And make it good and great, thou hast the art.
But, ah, I fear 'tis useless! I must sip
The cup of pleasure while 'tis at my lip,
And let the world go on its beaten way,
And with the selfish have my little day.
And should life bring the bitter, brimming cup
Of sorrow, I will try to drink it up;
And when strikes home its keen and piercing dart,
Perhaps I, too, shall have a better heart.
Till then I shall not be a saint, I fear,
Or fill what seems to thee a woman's sphere.

MR. SEYMOUR.

Well, here comes Clifton! So at once I yield
The subject, ere I'm driven from the field.
I have no hope to make a convert now,
At least, until he's made his parting bow.

Besides, thou'rt just the woman he admires;
He's no ambition thou shouldst have desires
Beyond the pretty women of the world,—
To have thy toilet nice, thy ringlets curled,
With dimpling smiles that make thy face their home.
But hush!—"Behold, the Conquering Hero comes!"

[*Enter Walter Clifton, a man of wealth and fashion, and husband expectant of Miss Kate Walters.*

Ah, Clifton! Have a seat! Myself and Kate
Have just been holding quite a warm debate,
Which ends somewhat like this: that woman's grace
Depends upon a stylish form and face,
And that her only province is to make
Herself so fascinating, she can take
By storm, the heart of every man she meets,—
Her greatness measured by their sure defeats.
Dost like the portrait, Clifton? Does it suit?
Give us thy heart's ideal! I'll be mute.

CLIFTON.

Thou hast not given me time for sober thought.
But when a man has once been fairly caught,
He's sure the power by which he met defeat,
Must be of all the world the most complete.
Thine own experience must have taught thee this,
That to be conquered has sometimes its bliss.

MR. SEYMOUR.

True, I was taken captive years ago,—
I've had no wish for freedom since, oh, no!
But serious now, a truce to every jest:
How shall a woman fill her true sphere best?

CLIFTON.

Why nature points the way! A *man* is strong
To battle with the world. To him belong
The sterner duties. Woman was not made
For life's rough highways, rather for the shade;—
To soothe man's hours when weary with the strife
That meets at every step his way in life.
She who best makes her home a place of cheer,
Fills most and best a woman's higher sphere.

MR. SEYMOUR.

I grant her province there. She moves the Eve
Of her own Eden. We should sadly grieve,—
The poor lost Adams of a suffering race,—
If there we could not see her smiling face.
That first, and always first. When she assumes
The duties of a wife, when she presumes
To rear and mould the soft and plastic mind,
That with her own high nature is entwined,
No other duties should take place of these,
No other pleasures have such power to please;

The voice of her true love she should obey,
And cast the light to make their brightest day.
Though hard the task sometimes, and stern, that's given,
The mother finds reward enough in Heaven.
But is that all a woman's hand can do?
Must she but this one phase of life pursue?
Has she no thoughts and energies like man?
Has she not right to do what e'er she can?
To use the gifts of mind she finds most strong,
That lend her power to overcome the wrong?
What time her higher duties do not call,
What should prevent her doing good in all?

CLIFTON.

Thou surely dost not mean by such a plan,
That she should labor side by side with man?
Do just the work her fancy points to do,
Though course and rough, or radical and new?

MR. SEYMOUR.

I mean these powers to her of right belong;
To follow her own impulse deep and strong,
And choose herself employment; — take the pen,
Or brush or scalpel, side by side with men.
In short, do any work her heart deems good, —
Her right God-given. Am I understood?

Clifton.

Yes, yes, I think I understand thee now
Quite well enough, and yet thou must allow
A difference of opinion on this point;
I fear thou'dst find things sadly out of joint
With this, thy plan. To such a motley throng
No woman of refinement could belong,
And keep the charm that lies in her pure heart,
And all the sweetness of her winning art.
'Twill do perhaps for her to wield the pen,—
"Blue-stockings," though, are terrors among men;—
Yet I've no fancy that a wife of mine,
Among the literary world should shine.
'Tis apt to spoil the beauty of the home,
And then the stains of ink so sure to come
On her fair fingers. Better jewelled rings
Become white hands than any such foul things.
And faugh! to see a pretty woman stand
With keen, dissecting instruments in hand,
Dividing lung from lung, and bone from bone,
A perfect Gorgon, turning one to stone!
I must confess, I shudder at such arts,
Though she's been noted for dissecting *hearts*.
Next, in the pulpit thou wouldst have her place,
Or in a public hall expose her face,
Be merchant, or mechanic, at her will,
Perhaps at building ships might try her skill;

In legislative halls should take her seat,
While men should listen at Gamaliel's feet;
Nor pause until she'd grasped the reins of fate,
And ruled supreme, presiding o'er the State!

Mr. Seymour.

I think a woman's own good sense would guide
Her thoughts and actions, in a field so wide;
And being finer in her nature still
Than we, the finer posts from choice would fill.
Instead of going down to find her place,
Would elevate her task, and give it grace.
Men, termed the civilized, are half like Turks,
So apt to sink to level of their works;
But she perhaps might teach them to be wise,
To lift their labor up, and with it rise.
And mingling more with those of low degree,
Instead of growing coarse, would make them see
Her purity of soul, until 'twould shame
Their baser natures with its silent blame.
A true-souled woman with a purpose high,
Who draws her strength from native purity,
Can walk amid the darkest stains of sin,
Amid the direful sound of passion's din,
And winning words to hearts polluted speak,
Without one breath to stain her spotless cheek.
The true, the good, in woman never fail.

Dost doubt? go look at Florence Nightingale.
Who does not honor her heroic name?
It puts inglorious ease to deepest shame,
And that false fear that woman's skirts may stain
Through earnest work where vice and sin has lain.
Outside her home, a fearless woman then,
Amid the ranks of coarse and brutal men,
Shone like a watch-fire through the camp, when strife
Had left the wounded struggling back to life;
And smoothed the pain from many a fevered brow
That bends with grateful blessing toward her now.
And brighter grew her spirit all the while,
As each new wounded sufferer caught her smile;
And when the soldier kissed her shadow on the wall,
It proved her sphere triumphant over all.
Let woman like true heroine nobly stand
If needs be, with the scalpel in her hand;
It turns to balm, to win back life again,
That hand as soft to soothe the sufferer's pain.
No voice like hers to man was ever given,
To speak of hope, or point the soul to heaven.
And who can better teach of God above,
Than she who has a higher sense of love
Than man can know; in whose aspiring soul
Devotion in its richest anthems roll?
I say most earnestly, I think her place

Is side by side with man when saving grace
Is named; except her home, if there's one sphere
Where woman most belongs, I know 'tis here.
In private or in public, 'tis no shame
For her pure lips to speak God's Holy Name.
With all her power, wherever woman can,
It is her glorious mission to save man!

MRS. SEYMOUR, *smiling.*

We read, thou knowest, that Woman first of all,
In Eden tempted man unto his fall!
If but as punishment for that old crime,—
For which we've groaned and toiled throughout all
time,—
And to redeem her wrong, she ought to teach.
This proves undoubtedly her right to preach.
If she was first to drag Man from the skies,
Now, let her tempt his soul again to rise.
If done as easily as was the first,
With wicked men we'll not be long accursed!

CLIFTON, *laughing.*

Thou hast the argument! I'm forced to yield,
Not to thy husband, but thyself the field.
And though I'm not convinced, I bide my fate,
[*Aside.*
If thou wilt only be the tempter, Kate!

MR. SEYMOUR.

Well, well, we'll see. The world is growing wise,
Another age may prove what this denies.
It has been so through all the ages past,
Truth deified, though martyred in the last. —
But where is Bruce? He tarries somewhat late.

CLIFTON.

Ah, that's the very thing I wished to state!
'Tis quite in keeping with our talk to-night,
He called to ask my aid to make all right.
A friend of his, you know him very well,
The great reformer and fanatic, Bell,
Has found a prodigy; and so invites
A few choice friends to share in his delights.
It seems we've got a Poet, fresh and new,
And sudden as the northern lights, if true,
Who writes us books all crowded full of thought,
With power from unimagined helpers caught.
And not content with that, must improvise
Songs snatched all fresh and new from out the skies,
Until 'tis said the city's half awake.
I ought to hope 'tis true just for thy sake,
Because the Poet is a woman, helping prove
The very theory thou seem'st to love.

IDA.

Perhaps it is the same who wrote this book, —
This, Mr. Clifton! wilt thou please to look?
I'll wait till Henry comes — I'm sure he'll know.
I'm glad he's there! How I should like to go!
Do tell me more! Does she recite, or sing?
And from what power do all her talents spring?

CLIFTON.

You must excuse me. I but just now heard
The simple fact, and not another word. —
But Bruce is coming round; if not too late,
He'll be most happy every fact to state.
He's head and ears in love with these new things,
And every poet wins his offerings.

KATE.

Not more than Ida! Why, she's lost her heart
Already with this witch's written art!
If meeting the enchantress, who can tell
How readily she'll bow beneath her spell.
Perhaps she'd bind her with a chain of rhyme,
And all around her cast the fragrant thyme;
Perhaps her own mysterious skill impart,
Till Ida too would have her magic art.
How is it, Ida, would it suit thy taste,

With poet's starry mantle to be graced,
Till thousands hung enraptured on thy word,
And every spirit to its depths was stirred?

IDA.

It would indeed. I'm not like thee in jest,
I'd like it of all things in life the best.
I'm flying to have Henry come, to tell
If he has fallen, too, beneath this spell!

MR. SEYMOUR.

Well, here he comes! I hear him in the hall.
He little dreams how we await his call!

[*Enter Henry Bruce, a man of intellect, travel, and liberal views. An old friend of Mr. Seymour, and on terms of intimacy with the whole family.*

What recompense for having made us wait?

MR. BRUCE.

I beg thou wilt excuse me, though I'm late;
I've just been having what I call a treat,
And one that every day I may not meet.
I knew thou wouldst not miss me much — I come
And go like one who feels himself at home.
And as 'tis early yet, I just dropped in
To tell the news — let that excuse my sin!

MR. SEYMOUR.

By Clifton we have just been kindly told
You've been the Improvisatrice to behold;
And Ida thinks the same who wrote this book;
It lies beside thee there — just take one look!

MR. BRUCE.

The very same! I know not what to think
Of this strange woman; for she seems a link
Between the dwellers of the earth and sky;
I cannot fathom all this mystery.
I was told candidly by Mr. Bell,
Who's known her from her early childhood well,
That ever from her earliest days of youth,
She's borne the stamp of virtue and of truth.
And yet it seems untrue, that all unsought
The songs she sung were by her spirit caught,
And that the words I heard her lips recite,
Were fresh and new, unheard until to-night.
I thought the power *to improvise* had past,
Or lingered only in Italia last.
Old Scotia's minstrels long have sunk to rest,
The sod lies damp and heavy on their breast;
And this cold climate slowly fosters song,
Yet was the inspiration high and strong.
I heard in Italy those people sing;

To me some thrilling charms around them cling,
There's such a spirit of deep, wild unrest,
With which the heart that listens is impressed.
The music, wild but sweet, that fills the air,—
The words that in the music's richness share,—
And all fresh gushing from the hidden soul,
Where deep within, its living waters roll,
Like fountain leaping with its silvery spray,
In wild, fantastic, and spontaneous play.
No studied thought to fashion style or rhyme,
But free and gushing, fitted to the time.
Though ofttimes simple—songs from out the heart—
Yet has my soul when weary of cold art,
Loved better far this voice of Nature's child,
Its weird-like tones, its native genius wild,
Than all the words the world's famed poets sung,
When science, art, had trained their pen and tongue.
But this was richer than I ever heard;
A thrilling grandeur swept through every word.
At times the spirit seemed to soar away,
As if it knew the path to endless day;
And then the tones died soft and strangely sweet,
As if some echo caught them to repeat;
Then, springing upward with a sudden flight,
Flung back the shadows into blackened night.
Then came her recitations, full of thought,
As if the fire of genius she had caught,

And poured it o'er her words, until the heart
Sent back response to all its thrilling art.
It lifted one from each corroding chain
That bound the soul, and gave it strength again.
And that which in the whole I most admire —
She would compel the spirit to aspire.
And when she stood in simple greatness there,
With that strange smile the features ever wear
When lit with thoughts that soar beyond the earth,
Or when some latent power springs into birth,
With words that strangely on the soul could win,
I thought of Italy's far-famed Corinne.
Not crowned by mortal hand she stood to-night;
Yet wore it well, all queenly, royal, bright,
Thought's fresh, green laurel on her youthful brow—
I almost think I see and hear her now.

CLIFTON.

Just what I said! I knew thou wouldst go mad
O'er this strange spirit in mortal garments clad.
But candidly, I must confess, I doubt
That she pours forth such thrilling strain without
Premeditated thought; such things are strange,
And go beyond the vision's common range.
Is it not reasonable to suppose,
That she is artful, and, because she knows
Men love the marvellous, takes this novel way

O'er thousands' hearts to hold a stronger sway?
I know not why she has such sudden power; —
True talent springs not strong in one short hour.
This Bell may be deceived. He finds a spell
In every miracle. Thou knowest him well. —
And didst thou hear her speak herself of this,
Or where or how she found such power or bliss?

BRUCE.

I simply heard her say, for weary years,
With silent prayers and efforts, and with tears,
She sought for power to speak her thought in word,
Until at last her earnest prayer was heard,
And strangely answered. O'er her came a power,
Swift, sudden as the morning's coming hour,
And all her thoughts leaped up with sudden start,
Like life-blood flowing outward from the heart.
She says, the power e'en to herself is strange, —
Not yet accustomed to this wondrous change.
But all her soul seems looking toward the heaven,
In one thanksgiving unto Him who's given.

IDA.

And was she gifted in her natural mood?
And did she seem as one that's true and good?
Was she like mortal, fairy, witch, or elf,
Or did she look a woman in herself?

Bruce.

Not unlike others, modest in her guise,
A soul of goodness beaming from her eyes,
Yet nothing marked to tell the power within,
That, when aroused, so many hearts must win.
She'd mingle in the crowd, and scarce be seen,
With thoughtful face, and modest, graceful mien;
But when her harp is once within her hands,
And rapt, inspired, before the world she stands,
A glow spreads over all her face and brow,
Before which others can not fail to bow.
And in her eye is kindled burning fire,
As if 'twere filled with an intense desire
For something beautiful it caught afar,
And beams and beckons like a morning star.
It seemed as though some angel's presence shed
A glory over all, and round her spread
The influence of a higher sphere divine,
All through her being in pure light to shine.
I cannot think, like Clifton, that she played
A part most false, when such true words she said;
Her look and manner were too great, too high, —
If false at all, she was *herself* a lie.
Though strange, though still I cannot understand,
Yet as I see her, harp within her hand,
With that unearthly look that brighter grew,
I could not, if I would, think her untrue.

IDA.

I'd give the world to see her, hear her speak!
For this strange power with all my soul I'd seek.
Is there no way for me to reach this shrine,
And pay her homage? for this book won mine.
But then, how could she care for one like me,
When thousands flock her wondrous power to see?
And yet it seems, if I could see her face,
And in it all the living goodness trace
That I have found impressed upon this page,
'Twould give me strength and power, almost an age.
It made some chords within my spirit thrill,
That once awake, I know I cannot still.
And could I know her, even though but slight
The intercourse, it seems as though it might
Give strength to something in me that would speak,
That yearns, aspires, and yet is all too weak. —
Laugh, Kate! I do not mind; — I know I'm young;
Life's harp to me is only newly strung;
But I shall follow out this whim of mine,
In spite of that mischievous smile of thine.
I love the power that speaks of life within,
That wins the soul away from vice and sin;
And to avow my love I'm not ashamed,—
No, not if by the censuring world I'm blamed.
Now Henry, Father, do contrive to make
Some place of meeting, just for my poor sake!

BRUCE.

Well, that is quickly done. For, but next week,
Within some public hall she is to speak,
And thou canst see and hear her there, and then
In after-time perhaps may meet again.

IDA.

Oh, I'm delighted! I shall count the hours,
Until I see, and hear, and know her powers.

KATE.

Why, Ida! wouldst thou go to hear her there?
I'm sure I would not wish such joy to share.
I think a woman in a public hall,
The thousands round her to promiscous call,
To criticise her dress, — if 'tis with grace,
To analyze her form, her eye, her face,
And hand her name about in public streets,
Where every loafer, privileged repeats,
Lets herself down from woman's lofty sphere,
And *I* for one, would never go to hear.

MR. SEYMOUR.

Well, everybody to their taste; but I
The gifts of this strange being mean to try.
If destitute of power to wisely teach,

Incapable the soul's deep chords to reach,
I think she's out of place. But if she's power
As my friend Bruce proclaims for her this hour,
I think she's standing just where woman should,
When she has power to do the world a good.

CLIFTON.

I'll not discuss the matter o'er again ; —
My real thought, perhaps, might give thee pain.
Although I think 'twould bring to friend of mine
Disgrace enough, yet if thou wilt, she's thine.
Let each one to his own opinion cling,
And if she will, why, let her talk and sing!
'Tis naught to me. I only go my way, —
'Twill be forgotten by another day, —
While thou'lt go thine. And Ida, I expect, —
Nay, even now I think I can detect
The poet's power half lurking in thine eye, —
That thou this woman's skill will seek to try.
Now please to write some eulogy for me:
With thy vocation though I can't agree;
Yet should I kneel at any poet's shrine,
Depend upon it, Ida, 'twill be thine.
It matters little which is wrong or right, —
But I must go, so say to all, good-night.

[*Exeunt Clifton. Miss Walters soon retires.*

BRUCE.

What notions Kate and Clifton entertain,
Of woman's sphere! Of course, they would not deign
To step on such unconsecrated ground,
As that where public teachers may be found
In woman's form, though pure as drifted snow,
And though an angel's speech might through them flow,
To purify each spirit that might hear—
Because "they step from woman's lofty sphere."
And yet they listen with intense delight,
And countenance, applaud, night after night,
The Drama, in whose scenes must woman take
An active part,—half its attraction make;—
Women whose souls, not always clean and pure,
To virtue's paths the listener's heart to lure;
Women whose lips speak oft the fatal word,
By which some heart to vice at first is stirred;
Women who act ignoble parts, that shame
True woman's nature, without word of blame;—
Nor think, though immorality they hear,
That women *there* has stepped from out her sphere.
Or, if they think, care not, but clap again
The actors, pandering to the base in men,
To low and vitiated tastes; that smile—
And shame their better natures—at the vile,
Degrading passions in the human breast,

In virtue's garb by talent almost dressed.
I do not mean by this, that I ignore
The drama's true-to-nature, thrilling lore,
Or that I would demolish, in disgust,
The Stage,—though much it panders to man's lust;
For, rightly managed, 'twould prove mightier power
Than e'en the pulpit, in the present hour;
Because the clergy are too much inclined,
To space so limited to chain the mind,
And narrate facts, and coldly speak their thought,
While life and inspiration have been caught
By the true Actor; he, the facts, the men,
In voice, and look, and action, lives again.
The preacher carves the statue cold and still,
The actor with the living soul can fill.
One hangs a glowing picture on the wall,
The other, with true genius in his call,
Shall bid the figures from the canvas start,
And step forth men, with living brain and heart,
To thrill through eye and ear, and reach the soul,
Until he triumphs, victor o'er the whole.
If men would act the *Christ* on this same Stage,—
His life as pictured on the written page,—
And throw a truthfulness in every word,
As Booth stood forth, another "Richard Third,"
'Twould take such hold upon the gazing heart,
As seldom comes from any preacher's art.

Like Christ, the earnest actor then should stand,
With blood-stains in his side, and foot, and hand;
And in his power, the scene long passed away,
Should be enacted in the present day;
Till unbelieving Thomas, rapt, should cry,
"I do believe — like thee I'll live — thou'rt nigh."
There have been preachers with this thrilling art,
Who dared to touch with living fire the heart.
Paul must have been like this; such Luther was;
And every Whitefield from this fountain draws.
And in our day, the Beechers, Chapins, thrill,
And move, and sway the human heart at will,
Because their spirit glows through every thought:
Old creeds and doctrines, thus new fire have caught,
And burn and brighten on the hearts of men,
Until old manna seems like new again.
Let men like these tread this degraded Stage,
And reënact what's called the Sacred Page;
Let women, like our Jenny Lind, but sing
The songs of Miriam's daughters, now to ring;
Let others in our midst, whose pen has been
The bright interpreter of thoughts within,
O'er whom the star of Intellect has hung, —
Whose brightest rays are purity, — find tongue,
And act no part except the pure and high,
The Drama in the dust no more would lie;
But from the chains of vice and sin be free,

And upward spring to native purity.
There are some noble souls, I know, that now
Live Actor's lives, with lofty soul and brow;
Who will not, like the rest, degrade their heart,
But act their *lives* as nobly as their part.
I honor them; but round the Stage there clings
Such filthy rubbish from foul offerings,
Such fallen women, and such worthless men,
I seldom go to Theatres; and then
When some one worthy of a higher place,
With life and genius pure, the boards may grace.
The people are to blame; they should demand
The fallen Drama now to take a stand
Above the mass, and be the impulse given,
No more to drag toward hell, but point to heaven.
It might not pay the managers as well
(And so for gold they feed the flames of hell)
In its first start, but when the fires once burn,
Of Genius, pure, refined, the good would turn —
That now are kept so far by vice away —
And honor it, and help it bear its sway;
Until its clear and ever lofty tone,
Should move the people's hearts to claim their own,
And feel its power for good, to truth to bind,
Where now the youthful but a tempter find.

MR. SEYMOUR.

Thou'rt right. There lies the field for such great
good,
And yet, how thoroughly misunderstood!
The vile stand ready at its open gate,
The good, disgusted, leave it to its fate.
All wrong. And yet how hopeless seems the task,
To renovate the tastes of those who ask
For such vile trash; then coldly turn away
En masse,—like Clifton and like Kate to-day,—
With careless thought, without a noble aim,
And idly bow at pleasure's shrine; yet claim
An aristocracy too high, too grand,
To tread the ground where God's own martyrs stand,
Whose path through thorns is marked with sweat
and blood,
While sinners in high places men call good.
I almost thought I was severe to-night
To Kate, but now I think it was but right
Her father was a man of noble mind,—
She's like her mother, every day I find.
I've done my best. She's thoughtless, heartless
still;—
With her I have exhausted all my skill.
I grieve. Her father was my truest friend,
And on his death-bed begged of me to lend
My aid in moulding Kate's young, careless mind;

But all in vain, day after day we find.
And now she weds herself to one more vain,
Whose character is not without a stain;
But rich, and fond of pleasure, full of mirth,
Like thousands, she mistakes it all for worth.
Before two years are past, I fear she'll know
The pang of life's first, great, heart-crushing blow.

BRUCE.

Whoever marries Clifton, may expect —
Though at the first with flowers and jewels decked —
To find him selfish, arrogant, and vain,
And get at least their share of this life's pain.
'Tis well for her — the day her soul repents —
That nature gave her not that finer sense
Of right and wrong, and of life's noblest aims,
That of another such high standard claims.
It pains my heart to see a woman, fine
And delicate, whom God made half divine,
So keenly sensitive in feeling, thought,
By misalliance to the level brought
Of some coarse, brutal, and unfeeling mind,
That by strange spell is round her own intwined.
To have her noblest thoughts thrown back unknown,
Appreciative or responsive tone
Never awoke within his careless breast —
Perhaps considered worse her very best;

And see him drag her down to his low plane,
As years pass on, or know the soul's deep pain
Consumes the life; though breathed not one complaint—
Bearing its burden like God's chosen saint,—
Till weary of its martyr pathway here,
Like summer bird it seeks a brighter sphere.
It makes one wonder if a Higher Power
Can watch, unmoved, such bitter trial-hour;
Or if such "marriages were made in Heaven"—
I'm sure, God's sanction was not asked or given.

MRS. SEYMOUR.

It is most terrible to know the strife
So apt to mix itself with married life,
And when I see such feelings of unrest,
Half hidden, half exposed in many a breast,
I shudder at the thought of our escape,
And wonder how stern destiny could shape
Such bliss for us as only comes to few—
Two souls that met, and keep their love still new.

MR. SEYMOUR.

Ah, yes, while pity rises in my breast,
I'm yet more grateful we have been so blest.
May Ida be as happy in her choice,

If ever comes the time when her loved voice
Shall answer back to some fond, loving heart,
And from her home we see her steps depart.

IDA.

Now, father, now I shall begin to think
Thou dost believe I'm just upon the brink
Of matrimony; for thy words, thy tone,
Are sad as if I were already gone.
My head is quite too full of poets now,
At any other shrine than theirs to bow.
I must reread Corinne. 'Twas long ago
I saw the work. I will this moment go
And get it, and refresh again my mind,
Anticipating thus what I shall find,
When I at last this new Corinne shall see,
And listen to her words with ecstasy.

[*She passes into the library, that opens from the parlor. Bruce soon follows her.*

BRUCE.

I thought I'd come and help thee find the book,—
I don't believe thou'rt competent to look.
Parnassus' dust I know has filled thine eyes,
In this thy swift ascent to poets' skies.
Be careful! Pegasus is no safe steed;
He throws the rider who takes little heed;

And all Castalia's waters may be found
Still insufficient to assuage the wound.
Perhaps the Muse has visited thee; thy brow
Bears poet's seal, I see it even now.

IDA.

Ah, jest! I've found the book, and here it lies, —
That proves which of us two has better eyes.
And as for words about my skyward flight,
I'd rather fall, than *always* stay in night.
And if my soul could get, for once to drink
Castalia's waters, I would tempt the brink
Of any mount, however steep and high —
Despite the look I see within thine eye.

BRUCE.

What didst thou see? I do not jest, indeed!
I only wish my hand had power to lead.
Sit down a moment. Let us talk of this
Bright gift, that seems to thee so much a bliss.
I've often thought, when I have heard thee speak,
With such a burning glow upon thy cheek,
And such an earnest, radiant, soul-lit eye,
Of life, of poesy, and all things high;
And when I've seen thee sit all lost in thought,
As if some unseen power thy soul had caught,
And borne it from thy body's power afar,

With lightning's steeds, and thought's bright-burnished car,
That thou must have an artist's soul, and now
To-night I see it more on face and brow.
I know most unmistakably this hour,
That if thou wilt, thou canst rouse latent power
To answer to this ardent wish of thine.
Confess thy heart! thou canst confide in mine!
For I suspect that thou hast tried thine art
At writing rhymes—Ah, Ida, why that start?
Now tell me all; my interest is strong;
In thy heart's earnest wish I've seen it long:
And let me be in this to thee a friend,
And if I can in aught, my best powers lend.

IDA.

Oh, wilt thou? Then shall I feel truly blest;
For much and long I've tried, and yet my best
Has been so weak, so more than wholly vain,
I've often thought I'd never try again.
But then some new desire impels me on;—
I strive and fail again, as I had done.
I've always kept it secret until now,
Not even my dear parents would allow
To know, although it is the only one
I've hid from them since first my life begun.
I could write nothing worthy of a smile,

And so I kept it hidden all the while.
But now thou know'st the fact, I gather strength,
And feel as though I'd found a friend at length.
Thou couldst do much to help me, very much, —
Such help, oh, I have always pined for such!
Thou hast a critic's eye, at once to see
Defects that might be hidden quite from me;
Thou hast such true poetic taste to train,
Assist my own, I shall take heart again.
Such range of thought, of history, of fact,
And scholarship, and travel, would exact
A higher style than I alone could reach,
Without some mind like thine to train and teach.
And then I know so kindly 'twould be done
That I'd grow strong e'en with the censure won.
At least I can but fail, and if I do,
Thou must catch up the strain, and make it new.
I marvel much that thou dost never write
The thoughts that in thee shine like stars in night.
Perhaps to this true motto thou hast clung:
"The sweetest songs are those no voice has sung."

BRUCE.

The motto is most true. Those who have spoke
The words that into life the heart has woke,
No matter how the song may thrill and burn,
Though lofty souls in reverence to it turn,

Yet, deep within their souls in sweetness ring,
Songs richer, deeper far, they cannot sing.
To these belongs no Anglo-Saxon word;
The soul's dim aisles alone by such are stirred:
And only they with spirits just as fine,
Can catch these "wordless songs" almost divine.
As they who listen to some murmuring shell,
That in its plaintive melody will tell
Forever of its home, the far-off sea;
So soul speaks ever of Immensity.
No doubt the artist whom I heard to-night,
Whose words were filled with such a power and light,
Is haunted ever by a sense of pain,
Because her richest songs will still remain
In far unfathomed depths, yet sing for aye,
As if to mock, with rich strains far away,
Those she has caught and pours o'er others here,
With visions of a more melodious sphere.
And yet those very pains but serve to wake
Still richer gifts, far sweeter songs to make:
The power within that shames the work best done,
Is that which has most glorious victories won.
The grand Ideal gives the mind no rest,
Until a second work shall shame the best:
Thus drawing deeper ever from the fount,
Thus scaling higher still Progression's mount.
Yet, Ida, those who best succeed, and give

The world best songs, too apt in sadness live,
Because their greatest power gives them to know
Still richer wealth in mind's far depths below,
And feel the link that binds them to the Soul
From whence these powers through all their being
roll.
It is a solemn thing; for they, the great,
Stand at the portal of Heaven's open gate,
With bright effulgence ever pouring through,
While of its gifts their souls can use so few.
And yet 'tis not because I feared to use
The mind's rich gifts, that I would such refuse;
For nature gave me not the power to sing,
Though at such shrine I pay rich offering.
My songs are all in thought; I have no word;
Alone my heart by their rich tone is stirred.
But 'tis not so with thee; I watch and wait
To see thee enter at the outer gate.

IDA.

I can but knock; though I am more afraid,
After the words by thee so truly said.
But yet, I'm weary waiting in the cold,
And that perhaps has made me overbold.
The faint in heart shall never win, they say,
So I will not despair, at least, to-day.
And sometime when thou hast a leisure hour,

I humbly beg thou'lt test my want of power,
By reading just a few of my poor rhymes,—
That I've revised yet vainly—many times,—
To make suggestions and to criticise,
To tear them into shreds till each one dies.
Though at their weakness I feel deepest shame,
And dread the ordeal, yet thou wilt not blame,
But point to better things, till all my pain,
Though hard to bear, at last results in gain.

BRUCE.

You've little to expect from me, save this:
"Two heads are better than is one." The bliss
Of making one poor effort for thy sake,
And watching oft the progress thou shalt make,
Will be a greater favor given me,
Than all the little good I do for thee.—
Why not to-morrow morning? I'll come in;—
Such pleasant task I'm anxious to begin.

IDA.

Thou'lt weary soon enough, I have no doubt,
To find what foolishness I've been about.
But any time, it matters not how soon;—
I fear I'll lose my confidence ere noon,
And have such dread to meet my critic's face
I'll lock my papers closer in their place.

BRUCE.

Then I'll come early. I've no wish to lose
This promised treat; and then thou canst but choose
Fulfil engagements made in such good truth,
Lest I should hold responsible, insooth.
Fearing another moment thou'lt relent,
I'll thank thee for this hour so richly spent,
And say, good-night. May pleasant dreams be shed
Through all thy soul — leave blessings on thy head!

[*He passes into the parlor as Ida retires, and finds Mr. Seymour alone.*

MR. SEYMOUR.

Well, Bruce, with eyes of both I think it took
Rather a tedious time to find the book.
With reading, I went fast asleep, I own,
And when I woke I found myself alone.
Sit down, my friend, 'tis not so very late, —
And then thou'st no one in thy home to wait.

BRUCE.

"No one to wait for me!" I wish I had.
Seymour, I think 'tis really quite too bad
That thou hast such a home, such happiness,
While I have none my heart or hearth to bless.
We grew up side by side, as schoolmates, boys,

Almost the same our interests and our joys;
But I have been a wanderer over earth,—
Culling,'tis true, oft here and there its worth,—
And now at thirty-five I cease to roam,
And find thee with a wife to bless thy home,
And such a daughter! If I dared to speak
The thoughts for which all words are powerless, weak,—
Can I presume upon our olden love,
To say without restraint, I prize above
All other bliss that life may have in store,
Thy daughter, whom I know thou dost adore?
And as I heard thee say to-night, dost dread
The hour when she, who o'er thine own has shed
Such light, shall bless another's heart and home.
I know with what bad grace these words will come,
And yet within my soul, since that first hour
I saw her face, has slowly woke a power
No other face or voice has caused to thrill,
A love intense, I have no power to still.
I've striven long to check this love, that came
So silently,—I have no cause for blame,—
Because I knew 'twould be so hard for thee
To yield her unto any, thus to me.
And she so young, so full of artless grace,
I cannot look upon her fair young face,
Without a pang. How can I hope to win

Her heart's first love? It seems almost a sin
To ask to wear in this poor heart of mine,
A flower so fresh, that seems so half divine.
I had resolved on silence, till to-night
Her mind awoke with such a glow of light
In our discussion, showing such a soul,
In whose rich depths I hear sweet anthems roll,
That all my heart arose with sudden power,
And would claim audience now, this very hour.
[*Pauses.*
Thou dost not speak. I shall not blame thy word,
Though all my soul unto its depths is stirred
With keenest anguish; for thou hast the right;
I hardly hoped for less than this to-night.
I do not know that I might ever win
One thought from her, nor would I e'er begin
That task, though ever hopeless it might be,
Until 'twas sanctioned by a word from thee.
No look or tone of mine has ever shown
Thy daughter that my heart was all her own.
I've closely guarded look and word, till now
I stand beside thee with an unshamed brow,
And say, that in thy daughter's hand must lie —
In her pure love, — my future destiny!

MR. SEYMOUR.

Pardon me, Bruce, that I have seemed so cold:
For thou thy thoughts so suddenly hast told,

And on this subject nearest to my heart,
I could not act the friend's, but father's part.
I did not dream such thought could e'er be thine,
That thou couldst love this treasured child of mine;
Thou, who hast seen the beauties of all lands,
To have thy fate in such a young girl's hands
Seems sudden, strange. Though with a father's love
I cherish her all others far above,
Except her mother, could I give her up?
Yet sometime, doubtless, I must taste that cup.
And now, I think there's not another heart
For which I would so soon with Ida part,
Or one that with such tenderness and truth
Would love and cherish her, and guard her youth.
If I, so young could think to let her go,
I'd yield to thee, if she, too, willed it so;
But hardly seventeen, a child at best,
Accustomed only to be loved, caressed,
She is not fitted yet to be thy wife,
And mingle in the duties, cares of life.
When she shall leave her home, the fond hearts here,
I wish her fitted well for woman's sphere.

BRUCE.

I did not ask that she should leave thy side,
Or dare to think of her as my fair bride,

As yet. I only hoped at best to gain
Permission, — though perhaps I give thee pain, —
To strive to win her young heart to my own,
Until it sends me back an answering tone.
If I but win her love, though long and late
Thou dost delay, I can with patience wait.
To see her, hear her voice, and win her smile,
Is happiness enough for me the while.
True love is void of self, it seeks alone
Another's happiness before its own ;
And if one feeling in my heart is pure,
This love for her is steadfast, earnest, sure.
I never bowed before at woman's shrine,
And why at her's I hardly now divine,
Save that I see in her pure soul a ray
To burn and brighten to a glorious day ;
And every look, and word, and act, reveals
The presence of a power my spirit feels,
Yet cannot clothe in words ; and over me
It casts a spell of peace and purity.
I came from Europe, sick of all the world, —
The giddy mazes where the people whirled
In outward joy, life's burning grief within,
Their best thoughts blasted with the fire of sin, —
A sad misanthrope. Joy's first morn was o'er.
I sought for peace upon my native shore,
But with no thought there could be joy for me ;

And in this mood I first encountered thee.
It took me back to childhood's early days,
It gave my heart its few first sunny rays;
But only when I saw thy daughter smile,
With that child-woman face, so free from guile,
My heart from its long lethargy awoke,
And morning's glory through my midnight broke, —
Not suddenly, but soft as comes the ray,
The first that ushers in the golden day, —
Until grown brighter with each added beam
That lit the sky with still a richer gleam,
Until all dazzling on my soul to-night,
The day-god rose with voice, "Let there be light!"
And shall it shine for me, give joy again,
Or will it only mock me with my pain?
'Tis not becoming that my lips should speak
The things of my own self, that thou might seek
In one who would make claim her love to win;
I only say, through my whole life I've been
A seeker for the good and beautiful in all:
I could not bear to let my standard fall.
And so, — though finding much of good in man,
Yet poorly carried out each noble plan, —
I grew more weary of my life each day,
Cared not how soon it should be swept away.
I craved a heart to answer back to mine,
And wake within me chords still more divine;

And finding not, as year by year past on,
My hope to find at last was wholly gone.
And yet I could not stoop as thousands do,
To win a love as base as 'tis untrue;
And so alone amid the crowds I stood,
Silent and cold, and never understood;
While in my heart still burned the living fire
That for some nobler life would still aspire.
And now, when I had closed my hopeless task,
When I had almost ceased such gift to ask,
I find a soul to give my own such rest,—
If with as fervent love I might be blest;
And I could shrine it in my heart of hearts,
With love undying, till all thought departs.
And could I win thy daughter for my bride,
She stands my equal: I have long defied
The laws that make the woman subject to the man—
A rule time-worshipped, but a barbarous plan.
From every thrall of mine as far she'd be,
As now she moves in her own purpose free.
Unworthy of the marriage rites the word, "obey;"
If love rules not, no other power can sway.
A woman of true spirit spurns control,
Yet when love asks, she nobly grants the whole.
This is the secret of thy happy life,
So high and free from all that petty strife.
I yearn for happiness like thine to share,

A look of calm content like thine to wear;
And I would ask no other boon but this —
Thy daughter's heart and hand — to bring such bliss.
And could I know such bliss would be my fate,
The time thou askest I would gladly wait.

Mr. Seymour.

Thou art most honorable. I know thee true,
That thou hast come to me, ere first thou drew
Confession from her lips of love to thee:
It has won thorough confidence from me.
I always knew thou hadst a noble heart,
And in this matter such a generous part
Hast thou now acted, that although I must
Take time for thought — excuse me, I'll be just, —
So sudden came thy purpose to my mind,
So closely round my heart she is entwined —
I bid thee welcome to my home and hearth,
As thou hast been to all its joy and mirth;
And when my thoughts are calm and free from pain,
Ere long, we'll talk this matter o'er again.
Meanwhile, of this be well assured, that none
But thee couldst speak such words as thou hast done,
And win a second thought, for doubly mine
In friendship's bonds thou wert, if she were thine.

BRUCE.

I take thy words. They bear a hope to me,
And there is one more chord that binds to thee.
Forgive the lateness of the hour; a spell
Has bound me here to-night, but now, farewell!

SCENE III.

Evening. A large public hall crowded with people of all classes. Mr. and Mrs. Seymour, Ida and Bruce, seated near the platform.

IDA.

'TIS near the time. I'm glad 'tis getting late.
In such a place, how tedious 'tis to wait!

BRUCE.

Yes, in such public gatherings every kind
Of influence meets, and every class of mind;
And with the busy tongues and moving feet,
'Tis seldom one finds comfort in his seat. —
I hope the entertainment will commence
Ere long, just to relieve thy heart's suspense.
Perhaps I set her gifts that night so high,
'Twill disappoint in the reality;
And yet I have no fear. Here lies the charm
Of every Improvisatrice, — in the calm
Or thrilling look of eye, and of the face,
The voice that catches some peculiar grace,
That sends the words home with such burning power,
They sway thee at their will, and charm the hour.
And then the thought that fresh from out the mint

Of mind, just newly-coined, — though seen in print
It must lose half its charm, — when one can hear,
Strikes home with such a wild-bird's note upon the
ear,
It seems as though the soul of one who sings,
Leaps sudden forth, and like a fountain springs
To meet thine own, and thou hadst caught the spray
Of real, living waves of song, the ray
Of golden sunlight over all outspread,
Wrapped like a glittering rainbow round thy head.
Here mind meets mind, fresh-gushing, young and
new,
The soul stands half revealed, if true, or if untrue.
Catch up these words, and write them on a page,
They're like a wild-bird drooping in a cage;
His song rings not so sweet and strong and clear,
As when through forest-aisles it met the ear.
There every tree caught up the wild notes sung,
And back again in richer sweetness flung.
Now, but the voice is heard, and in such hour
His heart sings not; there lived his greatest power.—
She'll enter soon; then judge with eye and ear,
Whether "she's stepped from woman's lofty sphere!"

IDA.

I wonder where Kate is to-night? Suppose
At party, ball, or theatre — who knows?

BRUCE.

Or Opera, — " Don Giovanni's" sung, —
I think we'd surely find her there, among
The town's elite, who are not apt to trace
The trail of vice when 'tis disguised with grace.
I love the music, but detest each word.
To-morrow night, 'tis " Norma,"—hast thou heard?

IDA.

I have not, though I read it with delight.

BRUCE.

We must be sure to go to-morrow night.
I'll ask thy parents now, — 'twill be so fine, —
If they'll consent to go, I know I've thine.

MR. SEYMOUR.

Bruce, Ida, hast thou heard those people there?
I think thy pet from them will get her share
Of vile abuse. Just list a moment, do!

STRANGER LADY.

I don't believe a word! It is untrue
To think it comes impromptu, without thought:
With such transparent sham I'll not be caught!

Young Gentleman, *with white vest, jewelled rings, and mustache.*

Perhaps she's beautiful, — would show her face:
Her fair white hand perhaps she moves with grace.
Who knows but I may fall in love, first sight,
And failing to win her's, may go bedight?

Young Miss, *with a simper.*

In love! I never thought thou hadst a heart.

Young Gentleman.

In justice then thou ought to give me part
Of thine. —

Stranger Lady.

I think it is a real shame!
I feel, myself, as very much to blame
For coming here to-night. If Mrs. Brown
Should know of this, she'd think us letting down
Our dignity, to mingle in this crowd. —
Such things as these ought not to be allowed.

Middle-Aged Gentleman, *with an air of careless indifference and mischievous look.*

I like to have the fun go on. I see
One and another look surprised at me,

And wonder much what motive brought me here.
But then I am not proud, like thee, my dear!

LADY.

Proud! No indeed! And so I find it hard
To make the people our true sphere regard.
But come alone hereafter, if thou wilt!
I'm sure, I hold it hardly less than guilt
To countenance such things; she may be vile,
And use this new-born power as artful wile:
No woman with a pure, unsinful heart,
Would in a public place take such a part.

MIDDLE-AGED GENTLEMAN.

Not quite so bad as that, perhaps, my dear!
There's so much said about a woman's sphere
Just now, perhaps she thinks she'll take a stand,
And make her woman's voice ring through the land.
Let's wait until we hear, and then decide,
Without regard to fashion, vanity, or pride.

ELDERLY GENTLEMAN, *with white neckcloth.*

Sir, at the best I deem it real sin,
For her to stand such public place within.
You know that Paul says, sir, "It is a shame
For woman publicly to speak." I blame
Her very much; and then I have been told,
She teaches such pernicious doctrines, bold,

As if she had no fear of God or man;
But I'm determined to defeat this plan
Before 'tis older; and I came to-night
To hear her words myself, and just indite
The heads. Next Sunday, I intend to preach
A sermon, to denounce the whole, and teach
My congregation of this deadly sin,
Before she can commence their hearts to win.
I mean to warn my people, sir, to stay
Within the fold, and not be led away
By such strange women, teaching stranger things,
Though with deceitful, siren voice she sings.
I'll do my duty, though it is a cross
To come, — in Heaven I shall make up the loss!

[*Sighs.*

BRUCE, *to Mr. Seymour, laughing.*

We have gone back to Pharisees again!
He thanks his God, he's not as other men.
No matter, truth will bide the test of all,
And by it let our poet stand or fall.
I hope he'll get a hit or two to-night. —
Ah, here she comes! They just turn on the light!

8

IMPROVISATRICE.

[*Enter Improvisatrice, preceded by an attendant bearing a harp. Intense silence in the audience. She leans over the harp a few moments, then raising her eyes toward heaven, touches the strings and commences singing.*

I seek no homage from the crowd,
Though hushed in silence long;
I sing at last because my soul
Will pour itself in song;
Because a fountain leaps within,
Whose ever-dashing spray
Can catch the light, and bear it back,
Like golden beams of day.

It matters not to me, the thought
That others round me fling,
When on this altar now I lay
My heart's best offering.
Far from the world I wrap me up
In robes that none can see,
And find true joy in Thee, my God,
If none shall smile on me.

I only care that other hearts
Should feel this thrill of mine,—
A chord electric that would draw
Each soul more close to Thine.

I only pray for power to break
  From every soul its chain,
A gift to win the tears that wash
  Away each guilty stain.

O human heart! that throbs and beats,
  So wrung with bitter grief,
Cast every sin from out thy midst,
  And thou shalt find relief!
When pure and clear as crystal shines
  The human soul shall be,
There is no place within its depths
  For such deep misery.

The light of heaven shall beam and burn
  Unto its depths below;
Through crystal walls it enters in,
  Like mist, dispersing woe.
And round its shrine for evermore
  The golden rays shall cling,
And through its aisles in thrilling strains,
  The angel, Peace, shall sing!

[*She pauses, leaning again upon her harp.*

[*Enter Attendant, bearing a letter to the Improvisatrice. She reads, exchanges a few words with him, and he then calls the attention of the audience.*

ATTENDANT.

It is requested by some persons here —
Who marvel much at this strange power, and fear
The songs thus sung are first prepared with thought,
And then committed, ready to be brought
Before the public in this novel way,
To exercise on all a greater sway —
That some one in the audience this hour
Themselves should give a theme, to test the power
Of this strange poet-songstress — something new, —
And if she sings at once, it proves her true.
She cheerfully consents, because 'twill prove
The truth of this strange art she claims and loves. —
The gentleman who gave me this request,
Will please step forward. Let it be addressed —
The subject — in a voice distinct and clear,
That every person in the hall may hear!

GENTLEMAN, *stepping forward.*

This power, so strange, seems hardly to belong
Except to Italy, the land of song;
And I must be forgiven, if I doubt
The power that brings these strange results about.
Though much I've heard of this strange singer's
power,
If she shall sing as readily this hour

From subject I propose, I will believe,
And as a truth at once the art receive.
'Tis this — I speak it with an honest heart:
"FROM WHENCE — WHAT POWER — HAS COME THIS SINGER'S ART?"

[*The Improvisatrice turns her eyes upon the audience, touches her harp, and without a moment's thought, chants in a clear, sweet voice, these words:* —

From the dancing rill
That will leave the hill
  For the brooklet far away;
From the mountain springs,
From the fount that flings
  To the sunbeam, crystal spray;

From the ocean caves,
From the foam-capped waves,
  From the shells and coral deep;
From the rock-ribbed shore,
Where the sad waves pour
  All their deep anthems loud and deep;

From the forest aisles,
Where the sunbeam smiles,
  And with flowers the sod is dressed;
From the shadowy vale
In the twilight pale,
  When the sun has gone to rest;

From the clouds that sweep
Through the azure deep,
  In their gold and crimson light;
From the starry eyes
Of the summer skies,
  That will shine because 'tis night;

Yes, from Nature's sod,
"Up to Nature's God,"
  Has the unseen power been given;
Till it led my soul
Through the mighty whole,
  To the gates of yon bright Heaven!

With each human mind
There's a cord entwined,
  And a hidden, unseen law;
That have given the power,
In each passing hour,
  From its wealth and strength to draw.

From the Angel band
In the summer land,
  Where the loved ones ever go,
There's a wealth of thought
By the spirit caught,
  When their inspirations flow.

There's an inner shrine
That is more divine
  Than a mortal eye can see;
And in all that lives,
There's a soul that gives
  Of its best gifts unto me.

When I'm most alone
With this deep unknown,
  Then the strongest is its power;
When my thoughts are pure,
Then I know 'tis sure
  O'er my soul its best to shower.

In the busy strife
Of this careless life,
  From my soul it hides away;
But it comes again,
With a low sweet strain,
  When my spirit bends to pray.

From my own deep soul
Do the anthems roll,
  Till they mingle with the rest;
Oh, many a mind
Has the power to find,
  For their heart, this welcome guest.

And my fervent prayer,
Is this robe to wear,
  Wherever I press the sod;
Then to bear it back,
In my homeward track,
  Unstained, to the giver, God!

[*She pauses enrapt, leaving the audience in breathless silence.*

GENTLEMAN, *rising.*

I rise to say that I believe no power
Had framed that song until this present hour.
My doubts on that point now are set at rest —
I think the owner of such gift is blest.

[*Resumes his seat.*

IMPROVISATRICE,

[*Leaving her harp and stepping forward, gives immediately the following, in recitation.*

Ay, blest! my soul is richly blest this hour,
That even one heart sees and knows this power,
And deems me truthful as I stand to-night,
And worthy of this golden shower of light.
I have no motive to deceive in this;
It could not bring my soul a greater bliss.
And as I see the eyes that look on mine,
And know behind them lies a soul divine,

That yearns forever of God's truth to know,
And fain would learn from whence all thought must
flow,
I could not stoop to give my soul to sin,
A thought of homage from this crowd to win.
I see some faces here whose thoughts I trace,
That think a public hall is not my place
Because a woman; others who would blame
And cast reproach unkindly on my name;
Others who know not what to think the while,
But half between their praise and blame, they smile;
And others still, who fear what some may think,
Though to their lips the cup they dare not drink.
But more than all the rest, through eyes, the heart
Of many kindly look upon this art.
To such my soul goes out in earnest speech,
Those hearts I know my words will soonest reach.
My fervent prayer is, may God's truth be given;
On motives true, I stake my hopes of heaven.—
What shall I speak to thee, my friends, this hour?

VOICE IN THE AUDIENCE.

Explain, as far as possible, thy power!

IMPROVISATRICE.

That will I gladly do. And yet no word
Can speak the power with which my soul is stirred.

For years I prayed for speech to tell the thought
That burned within my soul, with beauty fraught;
And though it thrilled my being with a spell,
I could not speak it, had no power to tell.
But in an hour when all was hushed and still,
My soul woke up with strange and sudden thrill;
It seemed, the voice of every greenwood tree,
And rill, and star, and wave, conversed with me.
And Nature stood revealed before me then,
In grandeur that I cannot lose again.
I caught new inspiration from the sod,
And in its voice I heard the voice of God.
And all the loved and lost seemed round me there,
More beautiful than Earth, like Angels fair;
That all through nature, voices called my name,
And these, my latent powers, obedient came,
Touched, quickened by the spirit of the night,
And beautified by angels of pure light.
Something within me sudden rose and spoke,—
The light of new creation o'er me broke;
And since that day my powers leap up at will,
And burn and quicken, all my being thrill.
And when I stand before thee as to-night,
All round me falls a mantle of delight,
And through my mind there comes a power divine,
As though superior minds were blent with mine;
Until to all its depths my soul is stirred,

And *must* find utterance in its song or word.
When song, the soul of Music comes to me,
Until each key is tuned to harmony;
Then like a prisoned bird it bursts away,
And with my song, I soar where all is day.
Yet my poor speech is faint and weak, compared
With that in coming time, which shall be shared
By others, better fitted for the power
That over me I feel bright Angels shower,
And spirits of the beautiful and free,
Through earth and heaven, that give in love to me.
This does but herald brighter things to come,
Before whose beauty shall the earth sit dumb.

VOICE IN THE AUDIENCE.

Dost think departed spirits give thee power?

IMPROVISATRICE.

I do. With Nature's voice that speaks through all,
With my own powers that in me ever call,
I do believe to me by God are given,
Strength, power and beauty, through the saints in
Heaven!

[*Excitement in the audience.*

VOICE.

Thou dost blaspheme! 'Tis infidel, such thought!

IMPROVISATRICE.

Then am I infidel! For I have sought,
E'en from a child, to win from Heaven a voice:
And now I've heard, my friends, with me rejoice!
And learn that all at last may see and know
Heaven's brighter joys, though living here below.
God has not made the two worlds far apart:
The loved shall meet!—Oh! thank Him from thy
heart!

[*Indications of disturbance in the audience.*

[*Improvisatrice, turning to her harp and lifting her eyes to heaven, chants with beseeching pathos and look of deep devotion, this Invocation.*

Sweet darling of the mother's heart!
Look forth from out thy Heaven,
And tell her with thy starry eyes
Thy presence still is given.
Look forth! and tell her God is great—
That He has opened Heaven's gate!

Fair maiden! fading in thy spring,
Laid darkly in the tomb,
Beam like a star from thy bright home,
Or flower in summer bloom.
Beam out! and say that God is great,
That He has opened Heaven's gate!

Loved mother! passing into night
  To leave thy darkened hearth, —
A shadow resting in thy place,
  For those thou left on earth, —
Look down! and say that God is great,
That thou dost wait at Heaven's gate!

Young bride! grown sudden chill and cold
  To one who loved thee well,
Who keeps thee treasured in his heart,
  Still binding with a spell,
Burst forth! and teach that God is great!
And pass to him through Heaven's gate!

[*A hush in the audience; many in tears.*

IMPROVISATRICE, *reciting.*

God's truth has ever been unknown to earth,
Because in way expected not its birth;
And gazing eyes, while looking for its light,
Have seen it pass, and called it cloud of night.
For this the true of earth have been defamed,
Their teachings false and infidel proclaimed,
While Error wears a robe of rainbow dyes,
And men exalt her proudly to the skies. —
But sometime Right shall take the place of Might,
And sometime day be ushered in from night.

Great Nature's laws men do not understand,
They break them wilful, trespass with high hand,
Or through strange ignorance sink deep within
The dismal gulf, the noisome cell of sin.
And when a voice says, "Thou shouldst be more strong,
Thus Nature speaks, and thou art in the wrong,"
Because 'tis something new, they have not known,
They answer with a sneering, scoffing tone.—
But sometime Right shall take the place of Might,
And sometime day be ushered in from night.

The soul that wins one gleam of light from heaven,
Can bear the sneers that men have ever given,
Can look unmoved upon a scornful face,
Can list a scoffing tone with angel's grace.
For in the soul a presence half divine,
Keeps ever feeding at the inner shrine
The light that burns with truth's immortal flame;—
All earth can never put that soul to shame.
And sometime Right shall take the place of Might,
And sometime day be ushered in from night.

So calm, unmoved, I stand, with waves of joy
Still sweeping through my soul: none can destroy
The angel Peace that sits with radiant wings
Within my soul, and ever sweetly sings.

No hand but mine can break the blessed spell,
And send her forth, at other shrines to dwell.
Oh human hearts! Oh eyes now turned on mine!
Hast won her yet? If not, oh, seek her shrine!
And then God's Right shall take the place of Might,
And then God's Day be ushered in from Night.

MAN, *rising in the audience.*

I am not satisfied with that one test!
The subject was familiar. Well her best
She might do with such theme. I give a new,
And if she treats that just as well and true,
Then may we well believe she has some power.—
I offer this, to test her gift this hour:
THE LIFE OF PERSEUS—HIS EXPLOITS AND SKILL.
Now let her answer, if she can and will!

[*The Improvisatrice lifts her eyes, and in a moment, a strange, beautiful expression comes over her countenance, and her eyes kindled as if the gods themselves came to her aid; then raising her arm majestically, she commenced the recitation.*

Perseus.

Son of a god. Great Jupiter, his sire,
To Danae came in golden shower of fire,
From his Olympus;—Danae captive there,
In brazen tower, and wild in her despair,
Beneath her cruel father's iron rod.

Ah, wonder not she turned to meet the god,
And gave him love for love. Her heart was riven:
He lit her midnight with the hues of heaven.
Beside his face all else was faint and dim,
And she forgot the world, herself, in him.
Thus Perseus was the offspring of their love;
Though half a mortal, yet he caught from Jove
Olympian fire, the lightning of the sky,
The power that carved heroic destiny.
Yet when Acrisios, his mother's sire,
Knew of the child, it roused his utmost ire;
For he had shut her from the world away,
Because the oracle had dared to say
That by his grandson's hand should come his death,
Determined in his day none should have breath
To thwart his fate. But Destiny's strong hand,
Relentless still in what the gods had planned,
Burst every band that mortal power could place,
And gave him one that bore a god's true grace.
With angry heart he sent them out to sea,
When all its waves were sweeping angrily,
In bark so frail he knew it would be driven
Upon the rocks, and their cold forms be given
To Neptune's caves, no more to visit earth; —
Destroying thus the danger of his birth.
And ere an hour was past, their bark was tossed,
And rent, and wrecked, and they had both been lost;

But when the Goddess of the Sea beheld
Their forms, her heart with pity swelled.
She sent the winds to rest within their caves,
And Neptune for her sake hushed all the waves.
She placed them tenderly in Ocean's arms,
Who bore them gladly far from reach of harms,
To that calm haven in the Ægean Sea,
Where Seriphos' fair island laughed with glee
To see the boy-god with his mother come,
Safe from all danger there to find a home.
The sad waves murmured when the voyage was o'er,
That they must turn and leave them on the shore,
Alone and desolate, and drenched and cold;
So twined the sea-weed in full many a fold
And chain, about each pure, white form,
To shield them from the coming, angry storm;
And decked with shining pearl and coral shell
Their sandy bed, until protecting spell,
And strange rich beauty all around them spread;
Then placed their richest gems upon their head.
And as the sea, impatient at their stay,
Called after them, could brook no more delay,
Turned toward their home, yet sent their mournful tone
Through all the isle, "Ah, leave them not alone!"
Good Dictys heard, and left his nets to dry,
And on them cast a kind and pitying eye,

And took them from their cold but gorgeous bed,—
While many a tear o'er their sad fate he shed,—
And bore them to the King, who saw the child
So beautiful, that on them both he smiled.

As years passed on, young Perseus grew in power,
And genius, prowess, till the fated hour
He came the King remembered with regret,
Grown jealous now; besides, he wished to get
His mother, Danae's love, hard to be won;
Yet most he feared the anger of her son.
So made a feast, requiring those who came,
In honor to his royalty and fame,
To each present him with a horse of power,—
Impossible with Perseus that hour.
Who, most unwilling to be 'neath the best,
Thus Polydectes in his power addressed:
"O King! I cannot bring the gift required;
Yet will I give what most thou hast desired—
Medusa's head. I know full well, O King,
It is to thee a welcome offering!"
The King most readily gave glad consent,
Because he knew if on such errand bent,
He must be slain. So bade him quickly go,
And though his mother's tears in torrents flow,
It needs must be. Young Perseus dried her tears,
With hopes of sure success assuaged her fears,

Then quick made ready for his bloody part, —
The gods assisting with their wondrous art.
They knew his innocence, and lent their power
To give protection in that dreadful hour;
For gods love most — 'tis said of old —
To help the strong of heart, the pure and bold.
Old Pluto came from his dominions dread,
And placed a helmet on his fair young head,
Which had the power to shield him from all eyes,
And Mercury gave him wings to thread the skies,
A dagger made of diamonds, sharp as bright,
To catch but not reflect the morning light;
While wise Minerva whom the cowards fear,
(To whom the enterprise was doubly dear,
Because Medusa, with the ocean-god,
Her sanctuary had unbidden trod),
Gave up her buckler to the hero brave,
That with its mirrored depths would wholly save.
And in her care he traversed air and sky,
Until he came to those strange Gorgons nigh.
Then did he need Minerva's wisdom, then
Her courage, valor, for the bravest men,
With but one look, by some deep power unknown,
The monster Gorgons could convert to stone.
He found them sleeping — the strange sisters three —
And knew this hour must speak his destiny.
He dared not look upon them as they slept,

For through their curling hair the serpents crept,
That never closed their eyes; at each slight sound
Their awful hisses through the caves resound,
That all the silence in strange terror breaks,
And into consciousness the sleeper wakes.
But with a firm, and still a dauntless heart,
He falters not until achieved his part;
And on the shield his eyes he's but to place,
To see it there — each monster's awful face.
Though frightful, — e'en its image brings a chill, —
He will not let it bend his iron will;
But without fear, without one thought of dread,
He severs instantly Medusa's head.
Then woke the sisters. Euryale sighed,
And Stheino groaned, and in despair she cried,
"What hand has wrought for us such utter woe?
From our dominion he shall never go,
But stand a statue, desolate and lone,
One look this moment shall transform to stone!"
The serpents hissed in concert with her word,
Until each hair with serpent life was stirred;
The caverns echoed to their heart-felt groans,
And sent them back in dismal, pitying tones,
Until Minerva pitied so their pain,
She made a flute to catch the mournful strain,
And give it back; that all the world might know
In what sad strains the deepest grief can flow.

Then Euryale, Stheino, sudden sprung
(While writhing serpents round their faces clung)
To find their foe, and with one look of hate,
And vengeance dire, forever seal his fate.
But Pluto's helmet hid him from their view,
With Mercury's wings swift through the air he flew,
Safe, safe from harm, and with him bore his prize —
Like meteor flashing through the summer skies —
Medusa's head ; while from each gaping vein,
The life-blood flowed as flows the summer rain ;
And where it touched the soil a serpent sprung,
And round the sands of Lybia's deserts clung,
To perish not ; but through all coming time,
To fill with poisonous breath the sandy clime.
Still on he swept, till, weary of his flight,
Amid the shadows of approaching night,
He passed King Atlas' palace where he craved
His hospitality, for he had braved
Great perils, and his spirit needed rest.
The King refused to welcome such a guest,
Because he claimed himself a son of Jove,
And oracles had said that one would prove
His foe, and rob him of his wealth and power ;
So gave nor food, nor rest, nor home, that hour.
And even sought to kill, until at length,
When Perseus saw his foe had greatest strength,
He held Medusa's head before his eyes:

One look!—then speech, expression, action, dies,
And monster-like he grows, until he stands
A mountain huge and high in Afric's lands.
Yes, stands there yet,—the mount still bears his
name,—
A monument to cast intensest shame
On those who turn the sons of God away,
And scorn and fear His truths the present day.

When morning came with bright and golden ray,
Young Perseus took again his homeward way
O'er Lybia's plains, until he neared the coast
Of Ethiopia, and he felt the boast
Of such exploit would Polydectes win,
To take him back to favor once again.
When lo! there met his eye a thrilling sight
That froze his veins with horror and affright:
A maiden, beautiful as morn's first beam,
Ay, fairer than a poet's wildest dream,
Stood, with the sunlight on her suffering face,
The very image of the purest grace,
Yet chained, chained to a rock, and from the sea—
While both her parents stood in misery,
Her mother, wringing in her wild despair
Her snowy hands, and pouring on the air
Shriek after shriek, with not one power to save—
A monster rose, and cleft the foaming wave

With his dread power, as he approached in wrath,
While breakers roared around his fearful path.
Just ready now to seize, devour his prey,
When, swift as sunbeam from the realms of day,
Down swept the hero. With one deadly blow
He laid the monster in his heart's blood low;
Then turned with tender hand and tone,
And rent the chains from her, the fair unknown,
And raised her fainting from the damp, cold earth,
While love from pity kindled into birth.
And when her parents knelt in fervent prayer,
And blessed him, rising from their dark despair,
Then, as the maiden silent by him stood,
Robed in the mantle of her gratitude,
That found no utterance save in blissful tears,—
Each one that fell to him yet more endears,—
Unable longer to conceal his love,
His eager thoughts that still to her would rove,
He spoke: "I love this maiden! If my bride,
No evil shall again her life betide;
I'd guard her in my heart by night or day,
Within my home in regions far away.
Let not my heart's best boon be now denied;
Say but these words, 'That she shall be my bride.'"
Then answered Cepheus, "It is better so,
That with her brave deliverer she should go
From danger threatening, lest she yet be slain;

That were indeed to us far deeper pain."
Then Perseus said, "Whence came this cause of grief,
From which, by chance, my hand has brought relief?"
"I caused it, I," said Cassiopeia then;
"For vainly boasting once and then again,
That she was fairer in her beauty's light,
Than were old Nereus' daughters, though so bright.
There came vile plagues in answer to my word,
Of which the earth before has never heard,
Until the people, in their fear and dread,
Consulted oracles that sternly said,
The plagues should haunt us, ever linger by,
Until this death Andromeda should die.
The angry god had chained her to this rock,
To wait and meet in terror such a shock;
But thou hast come and dashed this bitter cup
From her dear lips; we cheerful give her up."
Then Perseus bent his eye upon the maid,
And with love's own rich tone he softly said,
"Wilt go with me? thou art my destiny."
She only lifted up her tear-dimmed eye
To meet his own, then drop beneath its glow:
No need of words, the look best said, "I go."
"My brother Phineus has sought to wed
Andromeda," then Cepheus quickly said;
"He might assail thy life, and thou be slain,

So brave and good, my daughter chained again!"
"Ah, never fear," said Perseus boldly then,
"I have a power that triumphs o'er all men —
Medusa's head; one look transforms to stone;
And when I wed thy daughter, if there's one
That dares assail, I have but this to show,
And worse than slain he lies. I let thee know
This fact, that thou may'st tell thy friends to shun
The dreadful sight; its work is surely done."
Yet at the wedding feast the brother came,
From Perseus' hands his promised bride to claim,
And with his friends attacked the bridegroom there,
Who made a sign, then showed Medusa fair,
And each a statue turned, and kept his place,
With awful look of horror on his face,
To gaze on vacancy, cold, still, alone,
While Perseus claimed and bore away his own.

Arrived at Seriphos, how Danae met
Her hero-son! all passed her wild regret;
For fame had wreathed her laurels round his brow,
So nobly was fulfilled his earnest vow.
And with him came, fair as the morning star
That sends its beams from some bright world afar,
His cherished bride; her life seemed bright once
more,
And in her heart she said, "My griefs are o'er."

But Polydectes, still more jealous grown
Of Perseus' power, because so widely known,
Now sought his life ; till Perseus was compelled
(Though with the deepest pain his bosom swelled)
To show Medusa's head, and with its shock
Old Polydectes then became a rock.
And Dictys, who had saved them at the first,
And Danae after, from a fate accurst,
Was placed upon his throne by Perseus' power,
And all three turned and blessed him in that hour.
Then turning from his labors to find rest,
He drew his bride still closer to his breast,
Gave back his wings to Mercury again,
His helmet sent to Pluto's world of pain;
Then to Minerva for the power she shed,
Upon her Ægis placed the Gorgon's head.
And in the bliss he found within his home,
Resolved no more from its loved shrine to roam.
But soon Acrisios from off his throne
Was hurled, whose brother claimed it as his own;
And with true magnanimity of heart,
Brave Perseus chose to act a noble part:
(For though in childhood cast upon the wave
To perish, vengeance lives not with the brave.)
And hastening back to Argolis, he threw
His power against foul Prœtus,—him he slew;
And gave Acrisios again his crown,

His throne, from whence he'd cast the tyrant down.
Until the king, his grandsire, wept for shame,
And even more, that Perseus would not blame;
With joy and gratitude acknowledged then
His Danae's son with pride before all men.

Fain would we let the hero rest; but now
The Fates must be fulfilled; they break no vow.
So when one day performing some great feat
Of wondrous skill (with him none could compete),
The king, with admiration of his power,
Beguiled in happiness the passing hour;
As if some evil demon aimed the blow,
Some Fury prompted where the quoit should go,
It struck Acrisios upon his head;
At Perseus' feet he fell, alas! was dead;
That thus the oracle in truth might stand,
"That he should die by his own grandson's hand."
In vain was Perseus' grief, his anguish vain,
He could not bring him back to life again;
And mourning o'er his grandsire's tragic end,
Could hardly bear another hour to spend.
At Argos; hoping sooner to forget
The thought that filled his soul with such regret,
The deed to his true heart so half like guilt,
The city of Mycenæ then he built;
And ceased from mingling more in scenes of strife,

But with Andromeda he spent his life.
And from their sons came Hercules ; for fate
Designed that e'en his offspring should be great.
And even in his death he could not die ;
For those who loved him placed him in the sky,
With famed Medusa's head still in his hand,
And close beside him there his household band,
As constellations bright, with shining star
To beam for wandering feet from homes afar:
King Cepheus with his sceptre stretched in air,
And Cassiopeia with her golden chair,
Andromeda still chained, while Perseus nigh,
Seems hastening to her rescue through the sky.
And though 'tis but a myth in classic lore
Of Greece, coined in the ages gone before,
Yet under all its symbols, strange, absurd,
There runs through every allegoric word
A vein of truth, a beauty and a thought,
To bless the world when once that truth is caught.
He sprung through force combined of earth and heaven,
A mortal's heart, a God's true valor given.
Thus one true mind that's caught from heaven its fire,
Can therefore to its greatest powers aspire,
May thus win helmet, shield, and even wings,
And smite that Gorgon where each serpent clings;

Though Error is its modern name, one blow
From *such* an arm shall lay it sudden low.
It is because to few such power is given,
To few that Zeus comes down in fire from heaven,
That still Medusa lives, defies our power,
And can transform to worse than stone, this hour.
For his great valor passed he to the sky;
The ancients could not bear to see him die;
And as mid-heaven he holds Medusa's head,
The Galaxy around his pathway spread,
So bright and vivid in its richest grace,
While gleams a nebula to light his face;
And eight beside, the constellation bears,—
Terrestial light of heaven, at least, he shares.
So shall the soul pass into yonder sky,
That labors for the growth of purity,
With angels of his household, gleaming bright,
To share with him its stars, its power, its light;
To live forever, shining like the star
On earth's dark night, from its pure world afar;—
Celestial light to gild its pathway now,
And its own deeds a halo round the brow.
Old heroes, martyrs, saints, can never die:
Not always visible to naked eye,
Yet not the less the constellations burn,
Though mortal eyes to see them may not turn.
If *souls* could find a telescopic power.

They'd see them gleam through heaven this very hour.
But Herschels of the present day men hate,
Because they've power to see when bid to wait;
And if their eye detects a planet clear,
Before unknown, in God's celestial sphere,
And name it Truth, and number with the rest,
And feel themselves in this new knowledge blest,
The rest refuse to look, and call it vain,
And bid them act Galileo again.
But like the constellations, when the clouds
Have wrapped them in their darkest midnight shrouds,
They gleam as brightly on the other side,
And gild those clouds that their best power defied.
So truth shall gild old error's clouds of night,
Disperse her mists and shades with golden light;
And known at last shall be God's great unknown,
And man unshamed shall claim it as his own.
The truths of God I've found, till then I'll speak,
Though small my power, and though, alas! so weak;
And like the dew upon earth's flowers I'll lie,
Till God's great sun exhales me to the sky.

[*She ceased speaking, while her whole attitude and expression were an embodiment of her last words; and as she remained thus, many who listened almost involuntarily expected to see her float exhaled in a mist from their sight. Then suddenly turning to her harp, she softly touched its strings and sang.*

Sweet Peace! descend with noiseless wing,
  And seek each human breast,
And through the night in sweetness sing,
  And soothe to quiet rest!

Smooth every aching brow of pain,
  Till busy thought shall sleep,
Till morning light shall come again,
  Keep thou thy vigil, keep!

Good-night, O eyes that look on mine!
  Hope's golden dreams for thee:
May morning's hour bring joy to thine,
  As daybreak to the sea.

Good-night! My soul pours out its prayer,
  That Heaven's eternal light
May be the mantle thou shalt wear,
  Good-night, good-night, good-night!

[*As the last notes of the song died away, the Improvisatrice glided through the door of the ante-room and disappeared. The audience, after a moment's breathless silence, rise to leave the hall.*

MR. SEYMOUR.

Ida! in tears? I cannot blame thee, child;
Thou'rt not the only one her words beguiled.
I quite forgot myself in her strange power,
And thought Jove came again in shower of fire.

BRUCE.

The words, "delightful," "wonderful," I hear;
They've half forgot she stepped from woman's
sphere;
The magic of her words is on them now,
To-morrow, with a thoughtful, captious brow,
They'll find excuses for this glow of light,
And some, no doubt, can do it here to-night.
Hark! there's our friend the Pharisee once more.
Let's see what came to him from out this store!

CLERGYMAN.

I did believe this all a sham! She might,
Perhaps, have said each word she did to-night,
Without much effort, — needed slight enough;
I never heard from lips more trashy stuff, —
Except the last. Unless he hit a theme
She'd given out, it truly would not seem
She could compose so readily each part,
Because, besides her skill in this new art,
It would require a memory of names,
And facts, and skill that no one ever claims.
And I've no longer doubt she gets her power
From the Arch-Fiend; he knows how best to shower
His gifts, to lure, entrap, and to beguile
The hearts of men with all that's vile,
In guise of truth and virtue, as to-night, —

When once they're chained, he'll burst to sight.
I've heard enough. There are no words too strong,
With which to warn my people of this wrong.
It must be stopped! She'll make to vice a slave
Faster than I the souls of men can save!

MIDDLE-AGED GENTLEMAN.

Why so? With all the fiends, it seems to me
She ought to be less strong than God in thee!

CLERGYMAN.

True, true, but God sometimes permits such things:
And men hear best if but a siren sings.

STRANGER.

Well, let them sing! for such Circe as that,
I must confess, had chained me where I sat;
And I'm not conscious, even in the least,
That I the more bear likeness of the beast.
I think this modern Circe'll hardly charm
One human heart to aught that can be harm.
I never had my thoughts so raised to heaven,
Or such divine and noble impulse given,
To higher life or purer trust in God.

STRANGER LADY, *passing Mr. Seymour's group.*

I thought her dress looked really very odd!
Too plain. I think her taste is bad to wear

No ornaments, and plainly dress her hair.
She must be low, — so very little style!
And then her collar, who could help but smile?

GENTLEMAN.

Now I admired her dress, — so little show;
But I forgot it all in that strange glow
That lit her features when she turned to sing.
To-morrow night, Louisa I shall bring!

LADY.

Just like you, Ned! But what an ugly face!
I can't perceive where you beheld the grace.

TWO LADIES *pass as they leave the hall, talking.*

So much of comfort, joy, I have not heard,
As came to-night in that song's every word,
Since darling Minnie died. It seemed the spot
Was hallowed with her presence, — was it not?
Oh, could I see her, talk with her of this,
'Twould be such rest, and give me such a bliss!

IDA.

How can the world speak coldly of a voice
That bids the mourner's heart like hers, rejoice;
And with a look more light, condemn as naught
What seems to me must be from heaven caught?
Cold words and vain, grate harshly on my ear,

Just tuned to sounds from some far purer sphere.
Like the last speaker, how I wish to see
And hear her talk! Now, father, can't it be?
It might be done with ease, through Mr. Bell,
Her friend, I'm sure, because you know him well.
I should not dare to talk myself, but then,
To hear her once converse were joy again.

MR. SEYMOUR.

Oh, I'll arrange it, never fear for me!
Because, forsooth, I wish myself to see
This gifted woman; better comprehend
This new revealment, its true object, end.

MRS. SEYMOUR.

I cannot tell when all my soul has stirred,
As here to-night, with every thrilling word.
I wish to see her, too. The world may frown;
Thou knowest I'm not afraid of "Mrs. Brown!"

BRUCE, *as they pass from the hall to the street.*

How sweetly, purely, shines the moon to-night,
While over all like mantle falls her light!
It seems like fairy-scene; and such a hush
And stillness, after all this noisy rush
Of feet, I feel transported to a scene
Like that whence came the gift of this Song-Queen.

How can the hearts, so full of lofty pride,
And vain conceits, that all her powers deride,
Step forth into this shower of silver spray,
And not have pride and scorn all swept away!
Yet, if God's truth appeals to them in vain,
The sunlight of the spheres, that shines so plain,
The fairy moonbeam with its gentler art,
Can have no power to find their darkened heart.
See, Ida, how that star attends the moon!
So thou art following in her steps so soon,
To brighten still upon the brow of night,
And pour like her o'er other hearts thy light.

SCENE IV.

Evening. Mr. Seymour's back parlor. Bruce and Ida seated on a sofa, reading from a manuscript.

BRUCE, *laying down the manuscript.*

'TIS but a year sinee first I knew thy power,
Just then in bud, and now it blooms a flower
In this thy work. I'm proud to know it thine;
For in it thoughts of real beauty shine.
'Tis worthy publication. Let thy name
Go with it; thou hast sure no cause of shame.
I think the secret has been kept too long,
Now tell thy parents, Ida. This is wrong.

IDA.

I know; but I have wished my work to hide
From even them, until my best I've tried,
And something worthy their approval given;
And I have earnestly and hourly striven,
Because in this, as other things, my heart
Yearns in their sympathy to have its part.
Oh, I have worked so long to win their smile,
Still hoping, trusting, waiting all the while,
And now I'll leave thy judgment to decide

If this has aught to give a moment's pride.
The little good that seemed within its leaves,
Has vanished, thinking how the world receives
All but the best the poet ever gives,
And then sometimes approves not while he lives.
Besides, Miss Raymond's last, you know, has wrung
Praise even from the lips of those who clung
To that strange wish to do her talents wrong;—
She triumphs now; she has not waited long.
How can my glowworm's spark expect to find,
Beside her own, the notice of one mind?

BRUCE.

Her work is very fine. And, by the way,
I wish to read (I think I heard thee say
Thou hadst not read the whole) the sweetest thing
I yet have known her write or speak or sing.
But not till thou hast promised I may show
This to thy parents. 'Tis their time to know.

IDA.

Well, as thou wilt! If fitting that I should,
I humbly hope they'll find within it good!
[*Enter Mr. Seymour.*

MR. SEYMOUR.

Wrapped up in musty manuscripts, I see!
They're hieroglyphics, I suppose, to me.

BRUCE.

At least, they may not always thus remain,
Although long time in mystery they've lain.

MR. SEYMOUR.

Where is thy mother, Ida? — Ah, I hear
Her well-known step; I thought she must be near!

[*Enter Mrs. Seymour.*

Another poem from thy favorite, see!
I think it good. — Who can the author be?
Ida, I think 'tis time thou hadst begun
To try thy skill — why hast thou never done?
A year ago, Miss Raymond had such power,
I thought she would transform thee in an hour;
And now here comes another half as bright,
And yet thy muse still lingers out of sight.

BRUCE.

Please read the poem! That perhaps may wake
Her sleeping powers, and this long silence break.

MR. SEYMOUR, *smiling.*

I will indeed; for who of us can tell,
With my good reading, what might be its spell?

[*Reads.*

COME AGAIN.

BY CORA LEE.

The billows moan upon the shore,
In never-ending pain,
They sigh and weep forevermore,
"Come again, come again."

A maiden stands beside the sea,
Pouring her tears like rain,
And this her wail of agony:
"Come again, come again."

She watched a brave ship speed away
With white sails o'er the main,
Bearing her heart one summer day;—
'Twill never come again.

The summers come, the summers go,
She moans the same sad strain,
While with the waves her tear-drops flow,—
"Come again, come again."

And evermore the rolling wave
Pours out its deep refrain,
With her, bewailing still the brave,—
"Come again, come again."

A mourner stands on Life's bleak shore,
Calling in vain, in vain,

Upon the loved ones gone before,
"Come again, come again."

Time's billows beat upon the coast
Where she must still remain,
With sullen murmur, tempest tost,
"They will not come again."

The summers come, the summers go,
With her the same sad strain,
While with Time's waves her tear-drops flow,—
"Come again, come again."

The Angels heard her bitter grief,
And sorrowing o'er her pain,
They sung this song to give relief:
"The loved shall come again."

She raised her eyes from earth to heaven,
And, with this thrilling strain,
She saw her loved by whom 'twas given —
"We come, we come again."

BRUCE.

If thou wilt promise to forgive this sprite,
I'll tell thee now that Ida did indite
These poems; but disguising her own name
Through fears. Now do not therefore blame.
She wished for something worthy of her pen,
And waited for thy sympathy till then.

MR. AND MRS. SEYMOUR, *in one breath.*

Does Ida write these poems that we love?

BRUCE.

Her burning, tearful face I think will prove.

MR. AND MRS. SEYMOUR, *embracing her.*

My child, my child, how couldst thou thus deceive?

IDA.

Oh, my dear parents! hear me and believe,
'Twas but because I could not bear to tell
One thought, until I came to do it well;
Though I have pined for one approving word,
Which in disguise sometimes I've gladly heard.
But I have finished something just to-day,
Which Henry has the want of taste to say,
He thinks is good, and so I let him speak.

MR. SEYMOUR.

This gives me much of joy. Perhaps I'm weak,
But I have always yearned to see this child,
On which our warmest love has ever smiled,
Pursue a useful life, with cultured mind: —
In this beginning much of hope I find.
But what is this just finished — let me know?
No more refuse, my child, thy works to show.

IDA.

Oh, no indeed! It pays for all my sighs,
And fears, that 'tis to thee such glad surprise.

BRUCE.

Here is the manuscript. I think it ought,
Before the world, with her own name be brought.
I'll read some parts, then for thyself thou'lt see,
If this, thy daughter, speaks of hope to thee.
[*Reads several lengthy extracts.*

MR. SEYMOUR.

I'm not ashamed that child of mine should write
A thing like that,—it gives me joy to-night.
[*Draws her to him affectionately.*
Thou naughty girl! to keep this all from me.
I shall suspect some other mystery,
If this's the way thy confidence is kept;
I wonder how I could so long have slept.

MRS. SEYMOUR.

How could we think? for Ida's heart and eyes
Were always clear to us as summer skies.

IDA.

Forgive me this! I promise ne'er again,
In any mystery long to remain.

MRS. SEYMOUR.

But I'm not ready yet to meet our guest;
I must make haste. — My darling, be thou blest!
[*Retires.*

MR. SEYMOUR.

But Ida, tell me when thou first began,
And how, to carry out this secret plan?

IDA.

Two years ago, I first began to write,
But no one knew the fact, until the night
That Henry heard Miss Raymond sing at first —
The thought of her great powers my silence burst.
I told him all, because I saw 'twas vain
(For some way, all unknown, he caught the strain,)
To play concealment, and he promised then
To aid me in the efforts with my pen.
And well and truly has he kept his word,
I owe him much, for each has been referred
To his good taste and judgment, ere I gave
The little waif to float upon the wave.
And then Miss Raymond has been such a friend,
So always ready every aid to lend,
To make suggestions, criticise with care,
And praise my best — when I would half despair —
Without a jealous thought. It seems her aim,

To make me worthy as herself, of fame;
So unlike many, who, with envious eye,
Can bear to see no other soaring high.
She kept my secret faithfully the while,
Though she would sometimes shake her head and
smile,
And scold me for my foolish dread and fear,
But she shall know to-night; — she'll soon be here.

MR. SEYMOUR.

I always thought she had a noble mind —
Such lofty souls we do not often find;
But now I prize her higher still. She's done
What few would do for thee, my darling one!
And I will tell her how my heart is stirred
By acts of hers, that through thy lips I've heard.
On this, my child, thou surely canst depend,
That while I live, she never wants a friend!

[*Relapses into thought.*

BRUCE.

There's still an hour before she comes. Not late.
Let's read her poem — why not — while we wait?

IDA.

Yes, I remember thou wert now to read;
There's very little urging that I need.

[*They pass to the library.*

Ah, here's the book! I never shall forget
The first she wrote, or how her face I met.
It seems my soul from hers caught sudden fire,
And strength that would attain my long desire.
And then her hand has helped to feed the flame,
With thine; I hardly think I've right to claim
Much merit for my works, should any live,
So much I caught the light each mind could give.

BRUCE.

Why, every mind has deepest inspiration given,
When it approaches something nearest heaven.
And such a mind as hers is like the sun,
That sheds its rays — though swift its course may run —
To fall on others; they to catch the light,
As earth absorbs the sun's, and leaves her night.
And should the earth the radiant sunbeams spurn,
While still for light and power it ever yearns,
And say, "I dare not of another take,
For all my light within me must awake?"
Ah no! for God designed that sun to earth
Should send its beams, before the flowers have birth.
So mind with mind must meet and deeply blend,
Each unto each its inspiration lend,
Before the strongest powers to life awake,
And through the soul the beams of morning break.

Thou art no copyist. If through her light,
Some richer truths came forth to meet thy sight,
She has fulfilled her mission unto thee,
And thou thine own; and as for aught in me
That could inspire thy soul, would it were so;
It were such happiness that thought to know.
But I am prosy. Let me read thee here
What gives my soul such mingled hope and fear.

BRUCE, *reading.*

And yet there was one true and noble soul,
To whom she seemed for all his life the goal,—
One who had gazed upon her from afar,
As unapproachable as summer star
In its own azure; glowing with delight,
And shining for itself, and not his night.
Too fair a flower for his strong hand to take,
Too soft a harp for his rude touch to wake.

[*Bruce continues to read a lengthy extract from the book, descriptive of the progress of this attachment, that reveals points of resemblance to his own for Ida, and which, after many doubts in the minds of each, proves at last to be mutual. By this little artifice, he delicately prepares the way for a declaration of his love to Ida*

[NOTE.—After some hesitation, it was decided, while the book was going through the press, to omit here several pages found in the author's manuscript, in order to make room in the volume for several short poems, just brought to the notice of the Editor.]

BRUCE, *dropping the book.*

Oh Ida! could I ever win from thine,
Thine eyes or lips, such answering love to mine,
Then would my only wish on earth be given,
I would not ask for more this side of heaven.
Oh, I have loved thee long, — so very long,
With love, true, earnest, thrilling, deep as strong!
Nay, turn not from me those dear eyes away, —
I could not live without their cheering ray.
And this dear hand, oh, let it rest in mine
One moment, darling, with its touch divine!
And let me tell thee, ere thou dost decide,
How long I've prayed to win thee for my bride;
Since that first hour I met thy earnest look,
Unclasped for me a new and thrilling book.
I won thy father, ere I dared to speak
To thee, or thought of thine had dared to seek.
He will entrust thee to my love and care,
Oh, Ida! doom me not to feel despair!
At least, say thou wilt strive to win for me
One thought of love; — my thoughts are all of thee!

[*She buries her face in her hands.*

Continues, sadly.

And is there not one hope that thou canst give?
Ah, then how worthless is the thought to live!
Dost weep? Ah, do not! Let my hopes be vain —

'Tis better than to give thy spirit pain.
Now let me dry those tears, my happiness
Shall be to know that joys thy soul shall bless.
Ah, give me but one kiss to keep for aye,
When all my worshipped dreams are torn away!

[*He draws her gently toward him. She turns suddenly, and throws herself into his arms.*

BRUCE, *with deep and thrilling emotion.*

Speak, Ida! tell me, is there hope for me,
Who through these years have bent to worship thee?

IDA.

I did not think, I did not even dream
Of this; I only caught afar some gleam,
And thought Miss Raymond long thy heart had kept;
And if sometimes mine woke from where it slept,
I crushed it back; I thought it all in vain;
I would not listen to its voice of pain.
I am so young in life, in thought, while thou
Hast such maturity on mind and brow,
How could a wayward, thoughtless child like me
Be aught to fill the heart of one like thee?

BRUCE.

First, Ida, tell me that thy heart does love
Enough to give me time my own to prove!

First tell me, darling, that thou wilt be mine,—
Mine ever, as I must be wholly thine!

IDA.

I love thee more than any one beside;
But I, so young, how could I be thy bride?

BRUCE.

But thou shalt wait until thy heart shall say
With cheerfulness, the words for which I pray.
If I could know that thou wilt sometime bless,
Ida, I'd wait so long that happiness!
Ah, give me now thy promise with this kiss.
Enough! it comes to me, that word of bliss.
How can I love thee, dost thou say, so young?
I cannot tell; only my heart has sung
But this one song since first I saw thine eye:
"The morning breaks upon my darkened sky."
And, oh, to think that thou wilt be my bride,
And beam the day-star ever at my side,
That over me shall bend thy loving eye,
As clear and deep as is the summer sky,
That side by side, ay, ever hand in hand,
We'll journey toward the sunny, summer land,
Fills all my soul with such a peace and rest;
For all my wandering, now I'm more than blest.

[*Pauses.*

I hear Miss Raymond's voice. Though I would keep
Thee longer by my side, the fountains deep
Within my soul are strangely, wildly stirred
By those sweet tones from her, my singing-bird!
And I must let thee go, to calm thy thought,
And find the happiness in her thou sought.
But ere we sleep to-night, thou shalt be pressed
Unto thy sire's, thy mother's loving breast,
And feel their blessing on our pure love shed,
Descending in such peace upon thy head.
I'll take a turn or two upon the grounds,
And when my usual outer calm I've found,
I'll join thy group, with heart so full of bliss,
To cast the sunshine it has caught in this.

[*Embraces her and passes out, while in a few minutes after she enters the parlor.*

MISS RAYMOND.

Ida, as rosy as another Eve
Thou look'st to-night! In truth, I do believe
Thou has just bathed anew in some fair fount,
Or made a journey to Parnassus' mount.
I see the Muse reflected in thine eye,
Or something surely caught from some fair sky.
No wonder, for thy secret's out at last,
The god of silence can no longer cast

His mantle round thy lips; and now 'tis thine, —
The sympathy for which thy soul must pine.
Thy father has just told me his surprise:
I hope 'tis not his last before he dies.
'Tis better so. Now welcome to the field!
And I expect before thy power to yield!

IDA, *laughing.*

Ah, never fear! for I can only glean
Along the path where thou hast reaper been!

MISS RAYMOND.

Just hear the child! But we shall see, will see,
Not which will win the laurels, thou or me,
But which shall scatter best Truth's real seed,
Which most inspire to do the noblest deed,
Which strews the sunlight brightest on their path,
Which best dispels the gloomy clouds of wrath,
Which lives the truest life, with what is given,
Which marks with her own steps best path to heaven.
Ah, Mr. Seymour, how I often feel,
When all my heart goes out for others' weal,
What great responsibility must rest
On all by any gift of God so blest;
Sometimes can hardly bear the thought to live,
When I so little unto others give.
I've tried to do my best, and yet how small,

Compared with those bright gifts that round me fall.
I cannot catch them up, and give them clear,
In my own action, as in their bright sphere.
It makes me sad sometimes to think; and yet
I will not waste my time in vain regret.
Life is a school. To-day I'll try my best,
To-morrow try again, — so only blest.
But where is Mr. Bruce to-night? I thought
To see him here; indeed, I'm sure I ought.
I've business of importance to transact,
And to none else can I divulge the fact,
Unless he comes.—

MR. SEYMOUR.

I hear him coming now, —
So calm thy mind at once, and clear thy brow.
Don't keep us long in this suspense, I pray,
I'm dying now with what thou hast to say!

[*Enter Bruce.*

BRUCE.

Good eve, Miss Raymond! 'Tis a real treat,
Once more in quiet place thy face to meet.
I feared to see thee looking pale and thin;
I'm thankful 'tis not so. How hast thou been?

MISS RAYMOND.

Oh, much as usual! If I were but strong,
Had half the power that unto men belong,
To aid in carrying out my every plan,
I'd like it well. But then, I'm not a man,
And so am weak; yet sometimes one turns friend,
And then upon their strength I can depend;
And so I work. Now I've conspiracy
Well laid, to get a little help from thee.

BRUCE.

Well, name thy wish! I know but to obey!
A woman first or last will have her way.

MISS RAYMOND.

'Tis simply this: I wish, on Oxford street,
To open some good place, where all may meet
Of those poor creatures who are sunk in sin,
And see if something cannot tempt them in,
To hear such words as haply may unbind
The chains from here and there a suffering mind,
And win them back once more to light and truth,
And to the better feelings of their youth.
I want to get some good and noble souls,
Whose every heart-chord charity controls,
To meet and talk to them of all that's right
And noble in the spirit's truest sight;

And I will go and improvise in song,
And speak to them of all their sin and wrong,
And give such words as come to me each hour.
May not there be a hidden, latent power,
A gift spontaneous like my own might wake,
And burst the chains no other hand can break?
So much of real pity might be given,
'Twould tempt some feet to turn again to heaven.
To save but one such suffering Magdalen,
Were better than applause from tongue or pen;
For that will pass away in coming hour,
But such freed souls shall ever grow in power,
Still brighter through the years, and still more free,
A light for others through eternity.
Besides my duties, writing, speaking, all,
I could meet once a week. If I could call
A dozen good and noble souls like thine,
To help in such a work, 'twould be divine.

BRUCE.

I like it much; and I for one will do
All in my power to help this purpose through.

MR. SEYMOUR.

And I! I think it worthy of a saint,
To win such souls, and hush their sad complaint!

Ida.

There's naught that I can do, except to go
And cheer thee with my eyes, when there shall flow
The words I know full well to them will come,
To wake the memory of their childhood home.

Miss Raymond.

I'm truly glad my project takes so well.
Of course it meets the mind of Mr. Bell,
And several others. We shall soon begin
This work, and do our best to try to win.
We can but fail. But then we'll try again;
The noble only *seems* to fail with men.
God takes it up, and bears it onward still;
We cannot fail when we but do his will.
But who of us shall ever dare expect
To do great good, beginning with effect,
When with the men of wealth, of power, and fame,
And even civil power, oft lies the blame?
Night after night, in halls where gathering meet
To hear me now, the fashion, the elite,
I see such brows that wear the mark of Cain,
So many a soul that cannot hide its stain
From eyes intuitive; that through the day,
At God's or Mammon's altar kneel to pray;
Yet, worse than bandit, at the midnight hour,
Rob virtue, innocence, of all its power,

Then turn, and be the hypocrite once more,
And worship God as ardent as before.
'Tis terrible to see the tempted fall,
While God's own angels all unheard may call;
Their hours of suffering must be sharp and stern;—
"The way of the transgressor's hard," they learn.
But there's no law with such avenging power
To grasp their souls, as his, who, in that hour
Has been the tempter to their sin and woe,—
There is a Law that will not let *him* go.
He may escape the justice of the earth,
And men mistake his real guilt for worth;
Or through his wealth, or power, position, name,
May cast on others, and escape each blame;
Yet God has laws that none may e'er describe,
And judges that no man or gold may bribe,
Police who're ever watchful on their round,
Who see each act, and catch the slightest sound,
That never let the culprit 'scape his fate,
But hold to recompense,—yea, soon or late.
The tempter meets his doom. It matters not
Though thunderbolts may blast not on the spot,
Stern Justice binds him with an unseen spell,
And kindles in his heart the flames of hell;
And though he bears the sway in others' room,
There comes an hour when he must meet his doom.
I sometimes feel such bitterness to those

Who work for innocence such utter woes,
I cannot bear to see them honored stand,
But almost pray for God's avenging hand
To smite them from the earth, no more to be
Arch-fiends, with skill betraying purity.
Then comes the thought, I need not lift the rod;
They'll not escape the vigilance of God.
Such hearts I also seek to reach; for then,
Then only, when we have pure-minded men,
Shall woman shine like stars amid the heaven.
Must she stand strong, with all these tempters given?
Ah, well, we work not always as we would!
At disadvantage must we do our good,
And but a little when we would do much,
And still the greatest sins we hardly touch.
I should despair, only I know the drop
Of rain, will not for some great deluge stop,
But takes its place, perhaps in some flower's heart,
And is content to do its little part,
Instead of looking o'er the parching earth,
To say, How great the need! I'm little worth!
Let me refresh one flower, and not in vain
I live my hour; — I shall take heart again!

BRUCE.

Friends, we have dwelt upon this saddening sight,
Until from every face is gone the light!

Now let us bring it back, and keep it there,
To be the sunshine, still, for every care,
All ready to be poured o'er others' woe,
As healing balm wherever we may go.

MISS RAYMOND.

That's true philosophy! If we would give
To others sunshine, in it we must live.
Now, Ida, sing us something that shall bring
A blessing here, — bear healing on its wing.

BRUCE.

Yes, Ida, sing that little song of thine,
That Page set to his music so divine!

IDA.

Well, I will try to cast my little light; —
We can't expect to hear from thee to-night?

MISS RAYMOND.

Ah, no. To-night I take as time for rest,
And in this little group I feel so blest.
Now sing my soul to some bright, fairy dream,
Until I hear my native mountain stream.

[*Ida seats herself at the piano. Bruce follows to turn the leaves. She sings.*

Shine on me like a star from Heaven,
That trembles with delight,

Where on life's sea my bark is driven,
  Till I forget 'tis night.
Shine on me, till thy tender beam
Fills all my soul like fairy dream!

Shine on my soul! 'tis dark and dread.
  I find but midnight here,
Save in thy beams that round me shed
  A glory calm and clear.
Shine on my soul, until thy ray
Has made my midnight bright as day!

Shine, worshipped idol of my soul!
  Oh, give me love of thine!
And waves of joy shall wake and roll
  Through this lone heart of mine.
Shine, where no soul has shone but thee,
And be my type of Deity!

BRUCE, *in an undertone, bending over as if arranging the music.*

How thrills my soul to all that song to-night,
And trembles to its depths with sweet delight!

MISS RAYMOND.

How sweet the words! The music is divine!
For Page's fair brow the laurel yet shall twine.

BRUCE.

How pure the moonlight falls! 'Tis like the night
That Ida heard thee first with such delight.
Let's take a round on the piazza, do!
Wrap up in shawls, — the moon invites thee, too.
It is not colder than an autumn eve,
New strength and vigor we shall all receive.

[*The three pass out.*

BRUCE.

'Twas rich, — the scene, surprise, we had to-night!
Thou, too, deserved to witness such a sight,
When Ida's parents learned at last, through me,
That their own daughter was our "Cora Lee."
And I am glad the Rubicon is past; —
I hope she'll have more courage now at last.

MISS RAYMOND.

She must, she will. The world compels a strength,
When one is launched upon its waves at length.
With critics, flatterers, we must take a stand,
And though before we needed helping hand,
We grow by stern necessity to power,
Though as it comes we wonder every hour.
Thus Ida will be strong. Oh, how I shrank
From public notice, while at first I drank
Its turbid stream! But when the world once spoke

Its sentence, such a power awoke
Within my soul, enough to meet it then,
And stand uncaring at the sneers of men.
It gives the soul a broader view of life,
To be thrown out and mingle with its strife.
Besides, the world is but society the same
On larger scale, and bearing different name.
What matter if one town, or two, may speak
Of what is strong in thee, or what is weak?
Or state, or states, or hemisphere, or world?
One priest or ten, anathemas have hurled?
Nine critics or nineteen dispute thy fame?
Five presses or five thousand praise or blame?
I care as little for the thousands now
(And would no sooner to their mandate bow)
As once for personal friends. I bide my fate:
Through praise and blame the same I work and wait.
And Ida, when thou takest now thy place,
Let it be done with quiet, gentle grace;
But firm, unfearing, as the rock that stands
Where ocean-waves clutch at it with their hands.

IDA.

Ah me, I fear! and yet I feel more strong
Than when I lingered undecided long.
With two such friends and helpers at my side,
I ought the sternest tempest to abide.

BRUCE.

I know thou canst. The true and steadfast still
Must bow the world beneath their potent will.
It needs but one strong purpose that defies
The sternest power to crush that ever tries.

IDA.

Excuse one moment! for my cloak's too thin.
Is thine ?—I'll get some warmer, and be back again.
[*She enters the house.*

MISS RAYMOND, *looking after her and smiling archly.*

Confess now, Bruce, that with her magic art
Unconsciously she's stolen all thy heart!

BRUCE.

I do confess, Miss Raymond, that to me
She is indeed the "Type of Deity."
I loved her at the first, and deeper grows
The feeling in my heart, as on it flows.
And more than this, from her own lips to-night
I heard the words that give me such delight,—
That she returned my love, and sometime now
She'll be my bride. And I would tell thee how
This came, as thou hast ever been
Her friend and mine. — I feared I could not win

Her heart's young love, and doubted how to tell
The love in mine, lest it might break the spell,
And lose for me the confidence she gave: —
I must confess I was not over brave.
But in thy latest poem was a scene,
Where Morton won the love of Eloine;
Thou dost remember well the thrilling place —
I know it by thy earnest, speaking face.
I read that to her but this very night,
With heart divided between fear and light,
And caught the strength thy inspiration gave,
And poured my love out like an ocean wave,
And met return. Thou wert the helper, thou,
Thou knowest not half I owe thee, even now.
Thy help to Ida, thy unselfish love,
Thy noble nature evermore must prove;
And I shall ever claim my dearest friend
One who to her such helping hand would lend,
[*Smiling.*
Then wrote the words with which to win her heart:
Thou hast indeed a real magician's art!

MISS RAYMOND.

I'm truly glad that I can speak one word
By which the depths of other hearts are stirred.
This compliments my skill all else above,
If I can write distinctly others' love.

BRUCE.

If thou canst write of love so passing well,
Thou must indeed have felt thyself the spell;
Perhaps e'en now thy heart is not thy own,
Its very sweetness but another's tone.

MISS RAYMOND.

Ah, no, indeed! I never loved as yet.
Perhaps life's picture I might truer get,
Were such the case. But be that as it may,
I only hope beneath god-Cupid's sway
I may not bend; and yet I give thee joy.
In this thy happiness, may naught destroy;
But may the star of love but brighter beam,
And life be almost like a fairy dream!

IDA, *joining them.*

I'm here at last! commissioned though to say,
That none of us outside must longer stay;
For father says, in very piteous tone,
"The sunlight, moonlight, starlight, all are gone."

BRUCE.

I did forget myself! At once we'll go!
He will forgive us readily, I know.

[*Miss Raymond retains Ida a moment as they pass in.*

MISS RAYMOND.

Ah, Ida, I congratulate thee much!
Not every day can woman find one such
True soul as thou hast found to-day:
May blessings be on both thy heads, I say.
My two dear friends, how shall I love to see
The happiness that comes to such as thee!
He is like night, all set with stars of thought;
Thou art like morning when it first has caught
Aurora's beams: the two shall blend in one,
And day shall beam resplendent with her sun.
Ah, bless thee, Ida! May thine eyes be bright
As now they beam with Love's first sunny light!
Thy cheek as fresh with some glad thought within,
As now it burns in rosy light to win!
No tears to stain the roses in their glow,
No change but joys, to mark the years that flow!

[*They pass in.*

MR. SEYMOUR.

Well, Bruce, I think, has been most overbold,
To keep thee out so long in all this cold!
As long as moonlight gleams, he thinks 'tis right:
He'd never know if cold or warm the night.

MISS RAYMOND.

'Twas beautiful. — I had forgotten, too.
But now forgive us all, I beg, please do!

MR. SEYMOUR.

On this condition: that some one must tell
What conversation could have had such spell!

BRUCE.

Most readily. Miss Raymond says to-night,
She prays to never bend to Cupid's might;
That she has never been in love, not she,
And more than this, she never means to be.

MR. SEYMOUR.

Impossible! A libel all unheard!
I cannot think her guilty of such word.
Not wish to love, not wish to ever find,
For sweet companionship, some other mind,
So like and yet unlike, to meet and blend,
And higher, better powers through each to send?
Defend thyself, Miss Raymond, from the charge,
The liberty he takes is quite too large.

MISS RAYMOND.

Friend Bruce is right. I've nothing to defend,
However much I shock thee, my true friend!

MR. SEYMOUR.

Hast never been in love, nor wish to be?
If such is truth, do please explain to me!

Miss Raymond.

If I were not in such an element,
Where love seems current coin, uncounted lent,
I should say first, I don't believe in love,
Or if I do, in only that above,
Such as the angels feel who leave their heaven
To work for man on life's wild ocean driven.
But I must qualify. So little love I see,
That sometimes I have doubts if aught can be
Half worthy that pure name. For one true bliss
I find in such a family as this,
I see such agony and such unrest,
And such a bitter rankling in the breast,
That, sick at heart, I sadly turn away,
And think—"I'm sceptical of love to-day."
Just look at Mrs. Clifton! She, I know,
Has such an aching heart beneath her show,
'Twill not be long before her lofty pride
Will bid her wish, long years ago she'd died.
And thousands more that here I need not name
With but the happy few;—and where's the blame?
I must believe in marriage: nature speaks:
He who would fain evade, but vainly seeks.
Great Nature's laws are everywhere the same,
But someway in the meeting is the blame.
So much of ignorance, of self below,
So much of passion through false love will flow,

So much pretence, deception in the plan,
That I shall sure evade it if I can.
Let others love — the few as blest as thee;
My sympathy is theirs; but none for me.

MR. SEYMOUR.

I am surprised, Miss Raymond, at such word, —
From other lips all unbelieved if heard; —
With all thy gentle nature and thy heart,
To thus ignore this life's first, noblest part!
Why, woman's highest mission is to give
To others being, in her place to live;
To mould the fresh, young mind with her soft hand,
And place in other palms her magic wand;
To rear the youth to take his father's place,
More nobly fitted that he bears her grace.

MISS RAYMOND.

I grant it woman's place, whene'er she will,
This most important mission to fulfil;
But yet so painful, that the martyr's crown
To her belongs; for round her pathway frown
Full many a phantom that would sore affright,
Only she knows her path is toward the right.
I honor one who does this mission well; —
She binds me with her spirit's gentle spell,
And I sit reverent at her martyr feet,

As when the great of earth I chance to meet;
But still, I think her happiness is slight,
And that alone in striving for the right.
And I fulfil my mission, sacred, too,
The wrongs, mistakes of others to undo;
As far as may be, make another's child
More strong and beautiful, more meek and mild,
That otherwise had sunk in deepest sin,
But for some voice like mine, in time to win.
I choose in life from hers a different part,
Yet live like her, devoted to my art;—
To strive to do my good, to make the earth
My home, and wake to still a brighter birth
The souls I meet, unto my influence given,
And point them ever some bright path to heaven.
Like her, I'll take my life within my hand,
But unlike her, outside the hearthstone stand.
Yet, if I do, it is that I may shed
Light to more hearths than one, more thresholds tread,
And seek more hearts, and sweep them clean from sin,
And life, new life in virtue, help begin.
The gift that came to me, I'll bear for aye,
A sacred incense round my path alway;
And robed within it, I will pass along,
And seek communion with the soul of song,
And all things beautiful and fair and bright,

And scatter o'er the earth their morning light.
Forgive these words. Yet do I speak them here
Less strongly than in some far different sphere,
Where not the semblance e'en of love is borne,
And bitter sackcloth of the heart is worn.
Then could I pour my soul out in a strain
That now I will not; it would give thee pain.
God bless all lovers! say I unto thee;
But portion out, Oh fate, not one to me!

MR. SEYMOUR.

Thou'rt wrong, I think! but as thou wilt. Thy heart,
I see, is wedded only to thy art.
Perhaps 'tis well; and yet some noble mind
In thee such happiness would find!

MISS RAYMOND.

Not so! I do not always please myself!
I'm far from perfect — such a wayward elf!
And one that I could love, if such there be,
Would be as much dissatisfied with me.
When there's a *perfect* man, and *I am perfect, too,*
I think I might find happiness that's true;
But never until then. Myself I hardly bear, —
What should I do if two should be my share?

BRUCE.

Why, help each other bear! I frankly own
I should bear much to hear one loving tone,
To know one heart, despite my faults, was mine,
Despite its own, must lovingly entwine
Its destiny with that I bear, and be
A star of hope through all my life to me.
And would'st thou then refuse the sun's glad light,
Because a few dark spots would meet thy sight?

MISS RAYMOND.

No! but far rather I would bid it stay
In its own sky, so beautiful away;
Lest coming nigh, I could not help but trace
Other and larger on its now bright face.
And lest the sun itself, on coming near,
Behold but weeds where now the flowers appear;
Each small defect in noon-day glare would see,
And in disgust refuse to shine on me!

MR. SEYMOUR.

Hast thou no word to say in this debate,
My daughter? Dost thou, too, choose such a fate?

IDA, *blushing crimson.*

I fear I was but spoiled with so much love,
As you, my parents, gave. But time must prove

Whether I've strength to stand like her, alone,
And seek my joy in Art's profound unknown.

MISS RAYMOND.

But, see! 'tis getting late. I must away!
The carriage sure is waiting. Now, I pray,
Don't think me Amazon, or Gorgon, yet,
Lest in some after time thou might regret.

MR. SEYMOUR.

I'm only sorry that our sex can bring —
Not one among us all — an offering
That thou would'st wear upon thy heart, and say,
It shone the brightest gem to light thy way.
I do believe that thou dost hate our race,
Yet who could think it, with so mild a face?

MISS RAYMOND, *laughing*.

So far from that, I think so much of each,
I could not bear to their far sphere to reach,
And choose one to torment through all his life, —
So sure to be his fate were I his wife.
Now, Ida, I shall soon expect to see
Thy work forthcoming. Send the first to me!
Don't work too hard, and lose thine eyes' fresh light,
And now, though hard the word to say, *good-night!*

[*She passes out. Ida pauses with her a few moments in the hall, while the rest return to the parlor.*

Mr. Seymour.

It took me by surprise,—her sudden word!
And can it be she has her art preferred,
And ever will, to some true, loving mind?
So much of sympathy and help she'd find!
I wonder yet — I think it very strange;
It must be sometime all her views will change.

Bruce.

I think I can appreciate her soul,
It cannot brook the slightest earth-control,
But bursts forth free, impulsively, and strong,
To join with right, and wrestle with the wrong.
She springs, soul forward, like the hurrying wave,
The minds that others love to win and save.
Unless she meets, as meets the wave the rock,
Some noble soul, and the electric shock
Of thoughts congenial, as does the wave in spray,
Dissolves her theory in mist away;
She'll live devoted to her art, till life
Shall be no more, amid this care and strife;
But springing from the soil her foot has trod,
She takes her soul unstained again to God.
There are but few such souls; they cannot tread
The path that others mark; their course seems led
By some strange destiny to earth unknown;
Like some bright evening star they stand alone.

MR. SEYMOUR.

But few such souls, indeed,—but very few!
Whate'er she is, I know her good and true.

MRS. SEYMOUR.

Ida can never leave her; all her heart
Seems drawn to her, as hers to her pure art.

BRUCE, *with emotion.*

Not all, I hope! — My friends, I wish to say,
I won a hope from Ida's self to-day,
That my long, earnest love she could return,—
The greatest boon for which my soul can yearn,—
That if thou would'st consent, my bride she'd be,
And I would ask permission now of thee.

MR. SEYMOUR.

Then Ida loves thee, as I hoped and feared!
From but thyself, such words had hardly cheered.
But, as I told thee, unto thee we give
More willingly than to one heart that lives.
Only a year or two let her still be
A child to us, betrothed true unto thee,
Till she shall be a woman that can grace
Most true and fairly any woman's place.

BRUCE.

She can do that for me without an hour
Spent waiting; but thou hast the power
To thus delay. I would not now destroy
One of thy hopes, to sooner gain this joy.
Her love, her presence, shall my heaven be,
Her eyes the star of hope to beckon me!
And shall I seek her now, and wilt thou bless?
Before we sleep, seal this our happiness?

MR. SEYMOUR.

Go, bring her then! Thou hast from us beguiled
Her heart; yet we forgive thee, and our child!

[*Miss Raymond having just left, Bruce finds Ida in the hall, returning to the parlor.*

BRUCE, *clasping her hands in his.*

Come, darling! both thy parents wait for thee,
To give their blessing to our love and me!

[*He leads her into the parlor. She throws herself, weeping, into both their arms. They embrace her with words of tenderness. Then, Bruce taking her hand, they kneel before them.*

MR. SEYMOUR.

My children! may thy love be strong and sure,
Still burning clearer, ever growing pure,

So strong, no cloud can ever wholly dim,
But ever growing perfect, more like Him.
Cling closer when the tempest in its sweep
Has stirred the very fountains of the deep.
And should the hand of pain be on the brow,
Love only stronger than thou lovest now.
And through affliction let each chord entwine
Still closer, till thy love is all divine.
O Father! shower thy blessings on each head!
And when the buoyant days of youth are fled,
Oh, lead them gently down the steps of Time,
Through gates where Life Immortal stands sublime!

MISCELLANEOUS POEMS.

MISCELLANEOUS POEMS.

THE PEOPLE.

[" It is worthy of note that while in this, the Government's hour of trial, large numbers of those in the army and navy who have been favored with the offices, have resigned and proved false to the hand that pampered them, not one common soldier or common sailor is known to have deserted his flag. Great honor is due to those officers who remained true despite the example of their treacherous associates; but the greatest honor and most important fact of all, is the unanimous firmness of the common soldiers, to the last man. So far as known, they have effectually resisted the traitorous offer of those whose commands but an hour before they obeyed as absolute law." — *Abraham Lincoln's Message.*]

THE power is vested in the people;
  Though the men of office fall,
There's a mightier power behind them,
  Ready at the country's call.
Traitors may betray the Union,
  Brutus-like, may strive to kill, —
Men of office, politicians, —
  But "*the people*" never will!

Twiggs, like Arnold, stands a traitor,
  Armstrong sunk without a blow;
But our land has William Conways,
  To all treason, answering "No."

These are brave and these are faithful,
  When all others prove untrue;
Turns America unfearing—
  She has faith in such as you.

Floyd may fail, and e'en Buchanan;
  Bell may toll his parting knell;
Yet the banner of our country
  Floats as widely and as well;
For *the people* bear it onward,
  From the pine-land and the hills,
From the lakes and from the prairies;—
  We shall have a Country still.

Kings may boast their standing armies—
  Falling sometimes by their hand;
We've, thank God, a standing army
  In the heroes of our land.
Farmer, merchant and mechanic,
  Lawyer, millionaire, divine,
These shall make our *Stripes* a terror,
  These shall be our *Stars* to shine.

These shall teach to-day crowned Europe,
  Though may rise a traitor band,
That a country, through its people,
  Shall have power to nobly stand;
Shall maintain its institutions,
  That declare all men are free:
That *true power* lies in the people,
  Let all Europe turn and see.

Should the thoughts of truth and virtue,
Leave the courts and camps of Kings,
And the halls of Congress echo
Only to strange murmurings;
Should the men of office fail us,—
Virtue's sunlight overcast,—
In the true hearts of *the people*,
We shall find its altar last.

Socrates, one of the people,
Taught them truths that live to-day;
Christ, from his own humble Nazareth,
Swept the shades of night away.
Cincinnatus, grand through virtue,
Won renown in ancient Rome;
Wise, far-seeing, bold Columbus,
Found a world beyond the foam.

Pilgrim Fathers, when their rulers
Sought to bend them to their nod,
Grew a strong and mighty people,
Built a home to worship God.
Washington, from out that people,
Shone a bright resplendent sun,
Giving back his country's honors,
When its mighty work was done.

Abraham Lincoln, from the people,
Guides the Ship of State to-day,
"Like our Washington, O Father!
Like our Washington," we pray.

And the people, upward springing
At the trumpet's sudden blast,
He shall find them what he writes them —
"True and faithful to the last."

THE SOLDIER'S SHROUD.

HE lay upon the battle-field,
His forehead to the sky,
The death-damp in his matted hair,
And dim his glazing eye;
Embalmed within his own heart's blood
At Freedom's altar shed,
Among the heroes of that strife, —
The dying and the dead.

He lay upon the battle-field,
No friend nor loved one nigh;
He wrapped his banner round his form,
Most royally to die.
He bore it proudly in the fight;
A sacred charge 'twas given;
Fold after fold it floated out,
And caught the stars of heaven.

It led the way to Freedom's foes,
That patriot's eye might see,
And stronger grow at every sight,
The Flag of Liberty.

He bore it proudly, though the blood
  Was flowing from his side,
Though drop by drop his life went out,
  It floated in its pride.

He bore it onward, though his step
  Grew faint, and weak, and slow,
Still, still upraised ;—he could not bear
  To see it trailing low.
And when at last his latest power
  Failed, with his failing breath,
He fell amid its glorious folds,
  All shrouded in his death.

Had ever soldier better shroud,
  Upon the battle-plain ?
'Twould almost make the dead arise
  To bear it on again.
Had ever soldier better shroud ?—
  To him the stars seemed given,
To light the gloomy vale of death,
  And lead him safe to heaven.

He lay in state ; though but his foes
  Beheld him in his pride.
He lay in state : as if in death
  Their power he still defied.
'Twas sad to see his fair young face,
  So pale, so still, so cold ;
Yet could he well afford to die,
  Wrapped in that Banner's fold.

Brave soldier! if, in brighter lands,
Unto thy hand is given
The snow-white Banner, Flag of Truce,
Oh, bear it back from heaven!
And join our ranks, and let it float,
Till all shall turn to thee,
Till white-robed Peace, within our midst,
Joins hands with Liberty!

EMANCIPATION IN THE DISTRICT OF COLUMBIA.

Now God be praised! for this old world has moved;
Time's rusty wheels at last are newly grooved;
And our own country vibrates to the shock,
As when a mighty earthquake smites the rock.
It shook the Senate Chamber as it passed;
It echoed like a trumpet's sudden blast;
The time-stained White House with the voice awoke,
And Freedom stood erect once more, and spoke:

"No longer at my feet shall crawl the slave,
While high in air my starry banners wave;
No longer will I list their clanking chain,
Or on my garments wear this loathsome stain.
I stretch my hand, and grasp the power to-day;
When others fail, myself will bear the sway;
As when my sons declared themselves the free,
Shall beam once more the star of Liberty.

"In this, the District where my Temple stands,
I burst, indignant, every captive's bands.
Here, in my home, my glorious work begin,
Then blush no more, each day, to see this sin.
Thus finding room to freely breathe and stand,
I'll stretch my sceptre over all the land,
Until, unfettered, leaps the wailing slave,
And echoes back the blessings of the brave."

The Eagle hears her voice majestic given,
And down he sweeps like thunderbolt from heaven,
And, with a joyous scream, he makes the dome
Of our freed Capitol his future home;
Never to seek again his eyrie high,
To sit with drooping wings and scornful eye;
But ready at the call, to lead the brave,
Who shout, "Emancipation to the Slave!"

Ay, throw thy banners to the breeze of heaven;
From slavery's chain another link is riven!
Ring joyous chimes, as rung that bell of old,
Which once our fathers' "Declaration" told.
A few more roods of free soil has our land;
Our Capitol, at least, has room to stand.
Send one more bolt, O God, from heaven to smite,
And slavery cowers forever from our sight!

Not all in vain have lovers of the right,
Proclaimed true freedom in their fearless might;
Not all in vain the efforts of the brave,
To break the fetters from the bleeding slave.

Ay, not in vain on Slavery's sod is shed
The blood of our brave hearts, our cherished dead;
For, thus baptized, our soil shall all be free,—
The fruit of patriot's blood is Liberty.

THE AMERICAN EAGLE.

The Eagle sits with drooping wing upon the Southern coast,
With soiled and broken shield, the arrows from his talons lost,
The stars from his blue banner fled, the lightning from his eye;—
Old Eagle, by thy sons betrayed, dost think it time to die?

Why waits he silent on his crag, his eyrie on the height?
Has his keen eye grown dim with age, or blasted by this sight?
Hears he no clash of sounding steel, no tramp of armed men?
Down let him sweep, and lead to "Death or Liberty again!

But, lo! the North, that upward springs the Stars and Stripes to save,

With serried ranks, and glistening steel, and loyal
hearts and brave,
To hold the Union — leaves behind the patriot's cleaving sword,
The watchword of a Nation's might, its sacred household word;

And though that Northern heart is stirred, and though
its shout has rung
Through all the land, — 'tis not the song the patriot
fathers sung;
They shout "The Union!" evermore — "we'll stand
or fall for thee!"
The dying Eagle scorns to hear; *his* word is — Liberty.

The British Lion leaves his lair, and shakes his shaggy
mane, —
"America's proud bird will die — her sons be mine
again;"
And in his haste to seize his prey, treads down the
bleeding slave,
That, through long years of misery, has fled to him to
save.

The eagle opes his glazing eye, as comes the distant
roar
Of his old enemy, that wakes the echoes of each shore;
With ruffled plumage lists in vain for Freedom's battle-cry,
Then sinks; unlike his fallen sons, he knows his time
to die.

Proud bird! thou scorn'st to live,—tis well! Die
brave, and bold, and free,
Rather than live to symbolize aught less than Liberty.
When these thy sons shout other words, to wake thy
boding scream,
Perish the nation of thy love,—a vague, forgotten
dream!

Better America should die—her light forever set
Among the nations—than her sons that watchword
should forget;
Better her daughters die of grief o'er freemens' bloody
graves,
Than these her stars and stripes should float above her
million slaves.

Shout but the watchword, Liberty! and the old Eagle
springs
Back to his native power, and loud his piercing war-
cry rings.
His eye shall catch its ancient fire, then, Northmen,
only then,
Shall come his scream,—the tocsin bell of liberty
again.

Shout but the watchword, Liberty! Mount Vernon's
tomb shall shake,
Shout but the watchword, Liberty! and the whole
world must wake,
Shout but the watchword, Liberty! the spirits of the
free,

Shall leave e'en heaven to watch and write thy nation's
history.

Yes, patriots, martyrs, heroes brave, through all the
mighty past,
Who died for freedom, and around her shrine a glory
cast,
Shall break from their long mystic sleep at that one
word sublime,
And roll the anthem grand through all the corridors
of Time.

No! Eagle, in thy wounded pride, we pray thee die
not yet;
Thy glorious sun of liberty we pledge thee shall not
set;
America shall send her voice through all the listening
sky,
And call for "God and Liberty." Ho, Eagle! *scorn*
to die!

TEMPTER AND TEMPTED.

DEEP in the grave,
To sin a slave,
She went for rest;
Poor weary heart
That had no part
With aught that's blest.

The voice of sin
Had power to win —
  Her soul to blast;
No tears to flow,
Few cared to know
  Where she was cast.

She once was true
Young heart as you,
  And free from stain;
The tempter came —
With him the blame,
  With her the pain.

And yet the world
Its vengeance hurled
  On her so weak;
But took *him* in,
All stained with sin,
  With none to speak.

Well, let her die!
Forgotten lie,
  With none to weep;
Her tomb shall break,
A voice awake
  Her from her sleep;

And angel tears
Shall soothe her fears,
  And blot her sin;

And clothed in white,
Grown pure and bright,
She Heaven shall win.

O'er him at last —
Death's portals past —
Remorse shall roll;
A guilty stain,
The mark of Cain,
Be on his soul.

LET THE SAINTS BE GLAD IN HEAVEN.

Ah! let the saints be glad in Heaven,
And let them glory see;
But I will have still longer life
Ere I'll an angel be.

I care not for the heaven above,
I'll make a heaven below;
I'd rather walk an angel here,
Than all the angels know.

I shall not see the face of God,
If I should enter heaven;
So I will stay, and be like God,
And give the gifts He's given.

Then let the saints be glad in heaven!
And I'm rejoicing too;
If they are good and glorious there,
I'll be while here as true.

I care not for the golden harps,
I care not for the crown;
I'd rather scatter kingdoms here,
And put the tyrants down.

And if in white robes they may live,
And silver sandals wear,
And walk the streets all paved with gold,
And breathe a purer air;

I'd rather wear the garb of man,
And seek the lonely street,
Where I the child of poverty
And wretchedness may meet.

I'd rather have a step that brings
A joy at every tread,
Than all the silver sandals worn
By saints to earth long dead.

Then bring me life, an earthly life!
And let me live it true,
Before, O blessed saints in Heaven!
I come to join with you.

THE STOIC SOUL'S DEFIANCE.

All, all is dark! Ten thousand clouds
  Make pall-like all my soul,
And through its dreary, dismal depths
  The awful thunders roll.
Fate wraps me in her blackened shroud,
  The pall-cloth of her gloom;
And Destiny, with ruthless hand,
  Prepares me for the tomb.

Talk not of hope or joy, to me;
  It has a sound like scorn:
I curse the boon of Life! I curse
  The day that I was born!
Mock not with words of future life;
  I tell you, 'tis in vain:
Man sleeps a long and dreamless sleep;
  He never wakes again.

A few short days, a few short years,
  Of toys and petty play,
A few dark trials of the heart,
  And then he glides away.
And like a poor, degraded wretch,
  He creeps unto his rest,
With but one mantle o'er him cast —
  The sod upon his breast.

Forth out of darkness unto earth,
  A stranger does he come;
Like wanderer in a foreign land,
  He always pines for home,

And finds it not, unless in death;
His life, so short, so vain,
The only boon I deign to ask,
God, take it back again!

I scorn so mean a thing as life;
I scorn the Giver, too;
For, out of all His mightiness,
Man has not half his due.
And yet I scorn to thus complain,
'Tis base as this my life;
I will not stoop to mix me up
With all its petty strife.

I'll stand a martyr on the shore
Of time, my little day,
And bravely meet the surging waves
That bear my life away.
I'll make my soul too great to bend,
Too mighty to complain;
If there's no greatness in this life,
I'll find it in my pain.

I'll live a God the hour I live,
And like a God I'll die;
The mighty darkness of the tomb,
Unblenched my soul shall try.
And sing, with last expiring breath,
"Life gives but one thing grand —
Upon the voiceless shore of death,
In solitude to stand."

And put my bark from off the shore
  Into the silent sea,
With stoic scorn of this poor life
  My latest thought to be.
Ho! Giver of my life and breath,
  I cast it back once more,
Confront thee, standing in my strength,
  Till all of life is o'er!

CHANT OF THE SOUL.*

ACROSS the sea,
  Across the sea of Life I speed;
I look to Thee,
  I look to Thee, my God, in need.

I watch the waves,
  I watch the waves in ceaseless strife;
But Thou canst save,
  But Thou canst save, and give me life.

And in the storm,
  And in the storm, and clouds of night,
I see Thy form,
  I see Thy form, and all is light;

* As originally written by the author, and afterwards set to music by J. H. Crawford, of Oswego, N. Y., each stanza of the above poem contained six lines, repeating the first and third of each stanza in its present form, for the musical effect.

14

And hear Thy voice,
  And hear Thy voice low whispering, "Peace,"
And I rejoice,
  And I rejoice in glad release.

At midnight hour,
  At midnight hour on Life's wide sea,
I know Thy power,
  I know Thy power keeps watch o'er me.

And when most lone,
  And when most lone, from friends away,
I hear Thy tone,
  I hear Thy tone, "I with thee stay."

The waves may roll,
  The waves may roll, and all be night;
Thou'rt to my soul,
  Thou'rt to my soul its "Beacon Light."

And through the dark,
  And through the dark on Life's wide sea,
I'll steer my bark,
  I'll steer my bark straight unto Thee.

Though all the night,
  Though all the night so wildly driven,
At morning light,
  At morning light I'll enter Heaven,—

And furl my sails,
  And furl my sails on that bright shore,

Where stormy gales,
  Where stormy gales shall come no more.

And all my soul,
  And all my soul, like Life's great sea,
Like waves shall roll,
  Like waves shall roll fore'er to Thee.

THE REAL PRAYER.*

I STOOD within a shadowy-aisled
  Cathedral, vast and dim,
And listened to the organ's tone,
  Like a perpetual hymn.
'Twas not the time for service grand,
  When thousands gather there;
Only a few, with stricken hearts,
  Bent low in silent prayer.

The pictures on the walls were works
  Of some great master hand,
And bade the solemn past return,
  Like famed magician's wand.
And what a heaven was in the eye
  And face, upturned, divine,
Of that Madonna! Could one help
  But bow at such a shrine?

* A fact.

And, oh, the agony of him —
 The Christ upon the tree!
I turned away, — too much, too much
 Like stern reality.
And saint and martyr, bearing rack
 And torture for "His sake,"
O'er all the walls; enough it seemed
 The heart well-nigh to break.

I looked again at those in prayer,
 And said, "Who knows the heart?
Those pictures, like reality,
 Are but the works of art;
And may not these be pictured prayers,—
 The essence passed away,—
Devotion's form without the soul,
 The worshippers to-day?"

I paused in thought, and said, "Thy soul,
 Religion, tell me where?"
When through the open door there came
 An answer to my prayer:
A ragged little errand-boy,
 With bundle in his hand,
Walked silently, and knelt him down
 Where I had dared to stand.

He dropped the bundle by his side,
 And crossed his hands in prayer,
And lifted up his little face,
 A *living picture* there.

And what an earnest, speaking face!
  How eloquent the form!
Face, form, and ragged garments said,
  "God shield me from the storm."

Madonna, saint, and martyr-face,
  Faded like mist away.
"The past be with the past," I said;
  "Devotion lives to-day!
That look of earnest, trusting faith,
  No hypocrite may wear:
This poor, lone, friendless, kneeling child —
  The very soul of prayer!"

Day after day I've seen them kneel;
  Long prayers I've often heard;
But never one like that to me, —
  That prayer without a word.
And when I weary of the guilt
  That in devotions share,
I think of that young worshipper,
  And still keep faith in prayer.

THE RUINED CHURCH.

It was a sadder sight than one would think,
  To see that ruined church upon the hill,
Deserted, dreary, lone and desolate;
  But then its spire *would* point to heaven still.
Like standard-bearer wounded in the fight,
  Who, with his last remaining strength, upholds
His nation's banner; so this dying church,
  In its last hours, seemed bent on saving souls.

'Twas sad to see the windows broken through;
  But then they let God's air and sunshine in:
The church, once closed to keep all errors out,
  Now seemed as if it prayed more light to win.
And early spring-birds entered fearless there,
  Within the church-pale unconverted came,
And built their nests within the pulpit's shade,
  And never dreamed there could be any blame.

The door stood open; all might enter in,
  Jew, Christian, Heathen, Mussulman, the same;
As if, progressing even in decay,
  It held no creed that fashioned faith or name.
The pews were broken, doors had fallen off,
  The seats torn up, the plaster paved the aisles,
Strange names were written on the crumbling walls,
  And rubbish, panels, dust, lay heaped in piles.

I wondered if the ancient fathers slept
  In peace, within the churchyard just away,
While this, their pride, their consecrated dome,
  So all unheeded crumbled to decay;

And more, if creeds escape while churches fall,
If they've no broken doors and windows, too,
By time's or progress' hand,—through which the light
Of higher truths comes brightly streaming through.

I climbed with fear the staircase weak and old,
That tottered like a ship by tempest driven,
And wondered if the saints had feared as much,
When through its creed they groped their way to heaven;
And stood within the galleries that ran
From end to end, and bent and gazed below
With heart that trembled like the saints of old,
Lest all should crumble, and I "sink to woe."

And, as I gazed, and thought how sad that now
No feet of worshippers its old aisles trod,—
Alike forsaken by its builder, man,
And him to whom they gave, its owner, God;
I heard the voice of children in their mirth,
A group of little faces gathered there,
All unbaptized, some fresh from God's own hand,
Who played and sported where *they* knelt in prayer.

The scene grew dim; my eyes were full of tears:
Why ask for saints from those old days gone by,
When here come those with morning on their cheeks,
And heaven's own blue just prismed in their eye?
Those sunny curls an angel well might wear,
Those guileless hearts an angel's well might be.
No prayer that came from kneeling homage there,
Had half such music as their tones to me.

No sermon like their joyous, happy face,
  Their trust in all that comes, and is to come;
Their perfect love and absence of all doubt,
  Strike sceptic, priest, and pope, alike as dumb.
And who shall say they are not nearer Heaven,
  Than those old saints with all their "change of heart," —
These, fresh from God, just wandered out of heaven,
  Those, travelling back with theologic art?

I lingered till the human angels passed,
  Until the sun was growing faint and dim,
When, soft and sweet, amid the stillness there,
  The birds — Heaven's choir — began their vesper hymn;
And while I listened to their "Te Deum,"
  That made the ruin with its echo ring,
I said, "Not half so sweet the anthems loud,
  That many souls in dim cathedrals sing!"

And while this spire keeps pointing unto Heaven,
  And while the birds will build their nests and sing,
And while the sunny, blue-eyed children play,
  A strange, rich beauty to these ruins cling;
And I would rather wander there alone,
  Though by no worshipper its aisles are trod,
  To give my soul's deep homage unto God.

BEAUTIFUL SLEEP.

Beautiful sleep!
We call you, we implore you,
Come to us now;
Help us to rest the weary head,
From which the strength and power have fled,
And soothe the aching brow.

Beautiful sleep!
We kneel in prayer before you,
We pray you keep
Your watch around the bed of one
Whose work in life is scarce begun;
Oh, bid her not to weep.

Beautiful sleep!
Wonder not that we adore you;
For thou dost make
For mortals such sweet dreams,
That brighter each thing seems
Than in the hour they wake.

Beautiful sleep!
We pray you, we adjure you,
To bring your balm,
And round this soul thy mantle cast,
Till all the midnight hours are past.
Oh, shield us from all harm,
Beautiful sleep!

INTO THE DEPTHS OF HADES.

INTO the depths of Hades,
  Into its gloomy shade,
I'd go to find thee, loved one!
  Why hast, why hast thou stayed?
Didst thou not promise my own to be?
Hast thou not plighted thy troth to me?
  Wherefore then stay so long?

Wherefore then stay so long, love,
  Hiding away from me?
Had death but taken me, love,
  I would have come to thee.
I would have burst from its gloomy gate,—
Ah, when did I ever make *thee* wait?
  Oh, do not tarry now!

Oh, do not tarry now, love!
  My hair is growing gray,
While here I wait for thee, love,
  For thee, long years away.
Has that strange land been so bright to thee,
That thou in joy hast forgotten me,
  In thy bright home in Heaven?

In thy bright home in Heaven, love!
  Were I once safely there,
And thou on earth, no rest, love,
  I'd find, till thou couldst share.
I'd leave my white robe, I'd leave my crown;
My golden harp, I would dash it down,
  And find and bring thee home!

And find and bring thee home, love!
In Hades if thou art,
I'd share its tortures dread, love,
Rather than dwell apart.
For Heaven like Hades alone would be,
And Hades a Heaven, if shared with thee.
Then come, come back again!

SHAME ON THE COWARD SOULS.

SHAME on the coward souls that bend
At some such trifling thing,
And stoop from all their loftiest thoughts,
Such bitter words to bring!

Shame on the coward souls whose power
Is but in sunny days!
That faints, and dies, and fades away,
In sorrow's misty ways.

Shame on the coward souls that sink
Into themselves, when pain
Has seized them with a death-like grasp,
Nor gives them up again!

Shame on the coward souls that let
Some angry word disturb,
That know not on their haughty soul
To place the proper curb!

Shame on the coward souls that, when
They know full well their sin,
Wait, craven-hearted, ere the work —
Redemption — they begin!

Shame on the coward souls who've done
A known and wilful wrong,
Yet wait ere reparation's made —
Wait coldly, wait so long!

Shame on the coward souls, while here
In this first life they live,
Who learn not well that mighty work,
So Godlike, — to forgive!

Shame on the coward souls that, when
They've done a wrong or stain,
Shall seek forgiveness, and then soon
Shall do it o'er again!

Shame on the coward souls that seek
The beautiful and high,
Then sink below their better selves,
And fail when most they try!

Shame on the coward souls that wait!
Let them for once be strong,
And strike a death-blow swift and sure
To all within that's wrong!

ENDURE.

STRIKES it coldly on the heart—
Endure, endure, be what thou art?
Never bend beneath the load,
Never falter on the road,
Onward, proudly, through the strife,
'Tis the corner-stone of life;
Make your happiness secure,
Endure, endure, endure, endure!

Age on age must pass away
Ere earth saw the light of day;
Age on age must come and go
Ere she saw her waters flow;
Age on age be long gone by,
Life on life must live and die,
Ere her work was strong and sure,
Equal to endure, endure.

Nation after nation rise,
Standing,pointing to the skies,
Giving place to others still,
In the Father's mighty will;
Race by race must pass away,
Leaving naught to point the way,
Ere the soul is strong and pure,
Ready to endure, endure.

Trials dark must come and go
Ere the soul can learn to know
Of its powers to strive with wrong,
Hoping, waiting, working long.

Hope by hope must pass away,
Sorrows come to dim the day,
Ere the soul is strong and sure,
Powerful to endure, endure.

Let it be thy pass-word strong
While you wrestle with the wrong,
Write it deep within thy heart,
It will help to bear thy part;
Hold it surely in thy hand
When before a foe you stand,
And thy soul shall be secure,
Always ready to endure.

WENDELL PHILLIPS.

He speaks beneath his country's flag to-night,
Lover of Freedom, champion of right!
For years he stood outside that country's laws,
Yet struggled bravely in a noble cause;
But now he's seen where'er that banner waves,
Ere long to lose its stain, — the blood of slaves.
His heart of fire, and tongue of living flame,
Have burned the veil from off the nation's shame;
Those scorching words have lit a fire for thee, —
A beacon fire, O Goddess, Liberty!
Beneath them has old Tyranny awoke,
And shook and trembled at the truths he spoke,

Until she rose in wrath, and stands to-day,
To block the car of Freedom on its way.
It shall not be; true hearts like his stand strong,
And send their shafts to pierce the heart of wrong.

His was the heart unflinching in the storm;
His was the noble, almost godlike form
That walked the streets of Boston, in the day
When Freedom's sceptre half had lost its sway.
Then "Liberty's proud cradle" rocked her child
But roughly; Tyranny looked on, and smiled.
His was the escort that the great man wins,
Who dares to speak against time-worshipped sins!
The mob by thousands followed in his train,
And, but for law, that fearless form had slain;
Yet calm, erect, with Jove-like front he met
Those waves of men, till backward they were set.
Like some firm rock that still defies the sea,
Though years the waves have dashed most angrily;
Above the strife, its proud, defiant form
Stands all the same, alike in calm or storm.
But when our Northern blood had stained the street
Of Baltimore — foul Treason's work complete;
When Massachusetts sprang to avenge the stain,
Then WENDELL PHILLIPS could be heard again!
They pressed to hear, — the mob of weeks ago, —
Their hearts with patriot fire at last aglow;
At Freedom's shrine, they, gathering, bowed with thee,
Brave heart and strong! — then came thy victory!

We give thee welcome to our midst to-day!
Pour forth thy words till Freedom bears the sway

O'er all our land ; until no slave shall be ;
But all shall bear the seal of Liberty !

Launch thy "Phillipics" through the hearts of those
Who dare not meet the cause of all our woes !
Hold up the flag, until all hearts shall say
Its stars shall chase old Error's night away !
Let still the cry be, "Woe, forever woe
To all, until they LET MY PEOPLE GO !"

THE COMING TIME.

WHEN men forget their love of gold,
And love their honor more ;
When Truth is only current coin,
And counted o'er and o'er ;
When men love Freedom for *its* sake,—
For *all* as well as one,—
And for the greatest good, their work
From day to day is done ;
When men throw *self* aside, and live
For some great purpose high ;
Then will the glorious era come,
When none shall fear to die.

Then will the human soul grow strong,
And wise, and grand, and free,
Shall rise the coming race, O God,
A fitter type of Thee !

Then shall Thy seal, and only Thine,
  Be set on every brow, —
Ay, none shall wear the mark of Cain,
  As millions wear it now;
Then shall the Eden bloom again,
  Then shall the angels stand,
And with new Adams and new Eves,
  White-robed, walk hand-in-hand!

THE TRIAL.

The Past lifts up its solemn voice:
  America, it speaks to thee!
The blood of its old patriots cries,
  "Cease not till thou art wholly free!
Cease not, till broken every chain,
And all thy soil is free from stain!"

Thou hast no common work to do;
  'Tis for the coming years you bleed;
If thou art worthy of thy time,
  Each drop of blood is precious seed.
The fathers framed thy glorious plan,
Now thou must prove its strength to man.

Not yet must this Republic fail;
  For kings have wished long years to test
The "people's power," and see it fall.
  The hour demands it, — do thy best!
Teach kings and kingdoms what's true power,
By being equal to this hour!

No wonder that the red right arm
  Of battle, bares itself to thee;
God, may it never sheathe its sword,
  Till all our soil and souls are free!
Till in our midst no slave can stand,
Give us alone the avenging hand!

And when at last our nation springs
  At Freedom's stern, impartial call,
Proclaiming liberty to man,
  Sustaining "equal rights" to all,
Then, at the bondman's glad release,
May Freedom grasp the hand of Peace.

Ho, lovers of the true and right!
  The blood of patriots calls to thee,
From out their long-forgotten graves —
  The altars of true liberty:
"Cease not to pour thy blood like rain,
Till it has cleansed the nation's stain!"

THEY TELL ME THOU ART BEAUTIFUL.

They tell me thou art beautiful,
  Thy forehead white as snow,
While wave on wave around thy head
  The glossy ringlets flow;
And that thou hast an eye of fire,
  In which the soul of Song
Sits mirrored deep, around whose throne
  A thousand fancies throng.

That thine is such a queenly form,
  And thine such queenly face,
That every heart in homage bends,
  As in some sacred place.
And that this casket beautiful
  Holds something brighter far,—
A true and lofty, earnest soul,—
  As Evening holds her star.

I dare not meet thee! I might stand
  Heart-proof against thy face,—
And I might look, and but admire
  Thy dignity and grace;
But I should bend idolatrous
  Before thy matchless soul,
I could not catch its burning glance,
  And yet remain heart-whole.

I worship at the shrine of thought,
  Of genius, power and mind;
And well I know thy wondrous spell
  My every sense would bind.
I know 'tis weak—when comes the foe—
  And coward-like to flee;
But all have bowed to thee in vain—
  There's left but flight for me!

SERENADE—GOOD-NIGHT.

GOOD-NIGHT, good-night! the morning star
Is growing faint and dim,
And soon those choristers, the birds,
Begin their early hymn.

The Night has drawn his mantle close,
And turns to pass away,
And just behind him as he goes,
I see the foot of Day.

Good-night, good-night! for soon the beam
Will point from off the sun,
Like sceptre of a mighty king,
To say the day's begun.

And while the darkened shadows flee,
To leave their place for day,
I, too, with my dark, weary heart,
Like them shall pass away.

I've watched and waited all the night,
To look on thee afar,
As Morning waits through weary hours
To gaze upon her star;

But now I know no star for me
In beauty e'er shall rise,
To shine and send a glory through
The midnight of my skies.

For me there shall no morning come,
  For me there is no light;
Thou art my sun, — thou risest not, —
  And so, beloved, Good-Night!

"YE HAVE DONE IT UNTO ME."*

When thou hast heard the heart's lone prayer,
Low-uttered in its deep despair,
When sorrow called, and not in vain,
When thou hast sought the couch of pain,
To cheer the sufferer's aching eye,
And speak of hope, if they must die, —
Then angels bent to watch o'er thee,
Saying, "Ye have done it unto me."

When hearts are tempted unto sin —
If thou dost speak, their souls to win
From that dark midnight gulf of pain,
Making them strong and true again;
When wildly by the storms they're driven,
If thou a purpose high hast given, —
Then angels bend and watch o'er thee,
Saying, "Ye have done it unto me."

When thou dost firmly, strongly stand,
With earnest purpose in thy hand,

* Dedicated to Mrs. E. R. Crawford.

Though known, or though misunderstood,
Still striving bravely for the good,
Ready the power of truth to claim,
Though others put it unto shame,—
Then angels bend and watch o'er thee,
Saying, "Ye have done it unto me."

When to thy heart and to thy home,
Thy words have bid the wanderer come,
And watched with earnest, heart-felt prayer,
And with a mother's tender care;
When long-enduring, working long,
Through weary months, in purpose strong,—
Then angels bend and watch o'er thee,
Saying, "Ye have done it unto me."

When life's dark shores are left behind,
And Heaven's bright portals thou shalt find,
The angels, in their blest estate,
Shall open wide the golden gate;
And friends, and light, and joy, be given,
And all-enduring love in heaven;—
Then God shall bend and watch o'er thee,
"Saying, "Ye have done it unto me."

BURY ME UNDER THE GREENWOOD TREE.

Bury me, friends, where the flowers shall wave,
In the early spring, above my grave!
Where the earliest birds their songs shall sing,
And the lark toward heaven its flight shall wing.
Bury me under the greenwood tree!
'Tis the only place of rest for me.
I could not sleep in the dark, cold tomb,
I should pine in its mould, its damp and gloom!
Bury me, friends, where the violets grow,
Where close at my feet the brook shall flow,
Where the soft winds whisper among the bowers,
And the mosses sleep with the brightest flowers.
Bury me under the greenwood tree!
'Tis the only place of rest for me.

Come, when the flowers are in earliest bloom,
Come with the earliest spring-birds, come!
Come when the leaves are fresh on the trees,
And they softly sigh to the summer breeze.
Then every flower like my eye shall seem,
The song of the bird like my life's first dream,
While the whispers aloft in the leafy tree,
Shall all seem voices that come from me.

And do not weep for the dust that's laid
In the dim, cathedral, forest shade.
Think of me only as truly blest —
That I've found at last my promised rest!

Bury me deep in the forest lone,
Where only of Nature I'll hear the tone,
Where the foot of man has seldom trod, —
Bury me there, alone with God!

THE MORNING LAND.

They sailed from out the sunrise
  Into the light of day,
Into the blaze of noontide,
  With all its gorgeous ray;
Out of the night of darkness,
  Out of the house of pain,
Swift through the morning sunrise,
  Swift through the day again.
Sail on, sail on! Life's flowing river
  Leads forever to the Giver!
Sail on, sail on! thy bark must be
  Forever toward Eternity!

Into the silent darkness,
  Into the unknown deep,
Over the silent river
  Pass, and never weep!
On the shore there's waiting,
  Loved, to clasp thy hand,
Joys of the hereafter,
  In that Morning Land!

DEVOTION.

I WORSHIP at great Nature's shrine,
  Devout as any saint
That bows before the "great white throne,"
  The past has loved to paint.
My temple is the Universe,
  Its dome the arching sky,
Its lamps the glorious burning stars,
  The clouds its imagery.

The Ocean my baptismal fount,
  The "holy water" there;
The fruits of earth God's sacrament,
  And all may in it share;
The earth my Virgin Mother pure,
  To whom I kneel and pray;
Ave Maria! says my soul —
  She answers me alway.

The crucifix to which I bend
  Is God's own Bow of Light,
I count the stars, like Catholics
  That tell their beads at night;
The morning mist that graceful floats,
  And lingers on the hill,
Makes e'en the mountain seem to me
  A nun, white-veiled and still.

And, oh! the mighty organ grand,
  Whose countless thousand keys
Are scattered through the universe,
  And swept by every breeze;
How does my inmost spirit thrill —
  Spell-bound with magic wand —.
Beneath those grand and solemn strains,
  Waked by the Master Hand!

I join the hymn of Nature's choir,
  That binds me as a spell;
With Nature's Beautiful in prayer
  I whisper, "All is well:"
'Tis always Sabbath unto me,
  And hallowed is the sod;
One Priest is at the altar there —
  That Priest the living God!

WAITING AT THE GATE.*

I WAIT, I wait at the golden gate,
  That has opened and shut again;
My sun has set, it is growing late,
  Bright angels, O, take me in!
It has opened and taken the loved ones home,
And I hear them calling my spirit to come;
I am weary, heart-weary, as onward I roam,
  And would rest, — O, take me in!

* Written for Father Benjamin Gleason.

I gaze, I gaze on the golden blaze
  Of the clouds in a summer even,
Till they seem to me as the sun-bright rays
  That shine from the courts in Heaven;
Till they light my soul with a glorious gleam,
Till I fancy them dreams that the angels dream,
Till they fade, and the stars come forth and seem
  To my spirit as answers given.

I hear, I hear from the angel sphere
  A melody sweet and divine,
Till I know that the ones I love are near,
  That their spirits are singing to mine;
Till I long on the billows to float far away
Beyond the dark clouds and the sun's setting ray,
To the land of the Morning — Heaven's glorious day, —
  To thy home, thou dear loved ones — to thine!

I see, I see oft the Eden-tree,
  That is drooping with fruit most rare,
And I know it is waiting, ah, waiting for me,
  In its richness and splendor to share;
And my spirit, half-fainting, looks up and is strong,
For I hear the rich tone of the Seraphim's song
That murmurs in sweetness, "Not long, oh, not long
  Shalt thou linger in mournfulness there!"

Then I'll wait, I'll wait at the golden gate,
  Till it opens and shuts again;
Though my sun is set, though 'tis growing late,
  I will wait till they take me in;

For I know the bright hour is coming to me,
When my spirit will spring from its bondage free,
Through the golden gate I will pass to thee,
  Loved ones, and be taken in!

OSWEGO, August 9, 1859.

THE SOUL OF SONG.

SWEET spirit! that lives in my spirit's deep cells,
  And wakes into music each string,
Oh, touch with thy fingers my long silent lips,
  And bid them with melody sing!

I hear thy rich echoes forever and aye;
  They haunt all the depths of my soul;
I listen within to thy anthems sublime,
  And tremble and weep as they roll.

Oh, Soul of sweet Song! that shall live in my soul,
  And thrill in my heart-strings for aye,
Wake, wake to thy numbers my passionless lips,
  And set them to music to-day!

I dream of thy spirit such beautiful dreams!
  They haunt me in hours of my rest;
I hear thy low murmurs — a passionate wail —
  When my spirit is dark with unrest.

Oh! touch my cold lips as my *soul* has been touched,
  Till they speak of the grandeur within!
Oh! give me the power to repeat thy sweet strains,
  Or I die in the effort to win!

TAKE ME HOME.

OH, take me home! I cannot bear
  In this strange land to die,
With stranger hands to smooth my brow,
  And close my dying eye:

My mother through the weary hours
  Is waiting me to come;
I cannot die in this strange land,—
  Oh, take me, take me home!

The tones I hear are strangers' tones;—
  Familiar sounds and dear
Seem far away,—so far away
  They cannot reach me here.

Why, far away from that loved spot,
  Dear kindred, did I roam?
I cannot die in this strange land,—
  Oh, take me, take me home!

How can I rest within my shroud,
  That stranger hands should make?
How can I sleep within my grave?—
  My mother's heart will break!

The sun may shine upon that grave,
  The fragrant air may come;
Yet who could rest in this strange land?
  Oh, take me, take me home!

I miss my mother's hand to wipe
  The death-damp from my brow;
I miss the last grasp of her hand,
  I miss her strangely now.

Alone, I cannot find my way
  To Heaven's eternal dome:
Let me not die in this strange land,—
  Oh, take me, take me home!

WHO ARE THE BEAUTIFUL?

Who are the beautiful? They with a face
Gifted by nature with every grace?
They with a form termed faultless by art?
They are the beautiful, who own a true heart.

Who are the beautiful? They with an eye
Dark as the midnight, or blue as the sky,
Ever like magic on others to roll?
They are the beautiful who've wealth of soul.

Who are the beautiful? Those who are young,
And sunny and fresh, as the poets have sung,
Graceful and floating, and free as the wind?
They are the beautiful,—the noble in mind.

These are the beautiful: They that can stand
Nobly forever with heart and with hand,
Making thrice lovely the spot they have trod;—
They are the beautiful,—types of the God!

HARK TO THE WAVES THAT ROLL.

HARK to the waves that roll
Deep, deep within the soul —
Hear them sob and weep!
They mourn the silent dead,
For whom such tears are shed
In its fountains deep.

Its anguish who shall tell,
For loved ones gone to dwell
In their homes unknown?
Its weary waves repeat,
"We never more shall meet—
Evermore alone!"

O weary waves, find rest!
In regions of the blest
Must they live sublime.
O soul, be strong! thou'lt meet
The loved, in their retreat,
Far beyond all time.

MOUNTAINS.

I SEE them in their beauty once again:
The dear Green Mountains greet my eyes to-day,
Not black and bare as when they met my view
But one month since; but rich with foliage green,
As if they donned a festal robe to greet

My coming feet. How still the valley lies
Beneath their shade! as if protecting arms
Unseen, sustained it there, and gave it rest.
How every leaf, and flower, and tiny bud,
Looks up and smiles, and thanks the sun's warm
beams
That steal so lovingly into its heart,
To give it richer tints and fairer sheen!
And hush! the murmur of an unseen power
Is on the air, as if 'twere Nature's song,
The lullaby she sings unto her child,
When weary of the heat and glare of day.
There's such a music in the low-breathed strain,
So half unheard, that all my soul grows hushed
And still, beneath the strange, mysterious sound,
As if an angel sung. Each bough and leaf
Upon the tree, just trembles to the strain,
As if 'twere keeping time to every note,
Or possibly because the thrilling touch
Of this unseen musician stirs their depths,
And sets them all to music. Now there comes
A sudden breeze upon the grass, that waves
Its courteous salutation, as it goes
To touch Eolian harps among the trees
That guard the tall old mountain's breast,
Like serried ranks of men. How every string
Gives answer to the touch, and sends its voice
With stirring peal, deep home to every heart
That listens to the sweep, and stirs within
A stronger wish for action in itself.
It is as if a God had sudden passed,

And every tree grew conscious to its depths,
And bends its head in homage at the sight,
And trembles through the leafy veil of green,
With secret awe.
I love the Mountains grand,
For they have boldly stood confronting storms
And tempests in their wrath; and hurricanes
And whirlwinds beat their forms in vain.
They never cower when comes the biting blast,
Or shrink when storm-clouds wrap them in their
shrouds,
But rear their foreheads to the sky the same;
And when the cloudy veil is rent in twain,
Bright, living sunshine, like the smile of God,
Upon their summit rests. Alike in storm or calm
Immovable, fit emblem of the true
And loyal hearts that cling to truth and right,
Still firmly standing when the weaker fail,
And pointing, reaching still unerringly
Toward heaven. How can one human being live
Beneath their shade, unconscious of the truth,
The mighty lesson that they teach? How can
Disloyal hearts, disloyal to themselves,
Their God, their country, and their sense of right,
Grow up beneath their calm, unbending fronts,
And shame the soil from whence they sprung?
But few such souls find breath amid their wilds,
And they are aliens, even at their birth.
Old Scotia's Highlands reared such noble hearts;
Her crags and dells held eagle-hearted men
Who would not brook the foul usurper's power,

But made the Lowlands feel the hungry beak
Of those who thirsted for their freedom gone.
There Wallace dwelt, — her truest, bravest son, —
And lit the beacon fire that burned a flame
At last on Freedom's altar, once defiled,
But now swept clean once more from every stain.
And Switzerland's bold mountains bore a Tell,
As bold and as invincible as they;
Who woke the echoes of their dizzy heights
With Freedom's watchword; till the tyrant fell,
Pierced with a shaft from that Swiss patriot's hand.
And at his fall bright Liberty arose,
And stood erect within the citadel,
The rocky fortress God's own hand has made
To shield the brave.

Thank God! a thousand times
Thank God for mountains! They have ever been
The exile's home, the outlaw's safe retreat,
The last resort of God's old martyr-saints
When men had cast them out as heretics,
Closing the temple-gates against their forms,
And hunting them with rack and torturing art,
E'en to their death. The *Mountains* took them in,
God's grand cathedrals towering to the skies,
Within whose depths the ever-sweeping winds
Make grand and solemn anthems unto God,
That rise toward Heaven forever. Many a time
Have their deep, shadowy aisles at midnight woke
With pæans of pure praise from loyal hearts
That, cast from earthly temples, sought their wilds,
To pour the fulness of their hearts in prayer

To Him who casts them not away. What prayers
Have welled from breaking hearts amid their deeps!
What vows of vengeance have the mountains nursed!
What deep devotion has gone up from souls
To whom devotion was their life and light!
How many a houseless, homeless, wand'ring one
Has slept secure upon the mountain's breast,
Protected by its canopy of leaves,
And soothed to rest by its wild lullaby!
The martyr's bones are bleaching there unknown;
The living martyr-patriot nurses there
His wrongs yet unredressed, until his strength
Shall be sufficient for his utmost needs;
When, rushing on his foe like mountain stream
Just swollen by rains, he brings the power
That makes the Red Sea for their Pharaoh hosts.
When Freedom's altar is o'erturned, defiled,
Her emblems rent and stained with blood and sin,
When, wounded, bleeding, from her shrine she turns,
With tyrant blood-hounds howling on her track,
Her last retreat shall be her temple, built
Amid the mountain fastnessess by her
Own true and tried; the last to turn away
And leave her to her fate, the last to fail
In Freedom's cause, these hardy mountaineers;
The last to gather round her in her need,
And make a bulwark with their forms, and stand
Defending her till death.

Ah, once again
I welcome thee, old Mountains of my youth,
As thou dost welcome me, a wanderer!

I've been so weary since I saw thy face,
So faint with pain, and anguish, and distress,
So almost wild with fever's frenzied touch,
Heart-weary, sick of all the world, of life!
Oh, how I longed to have some friendly arm
Bear me away from that far stranger land,
And bring me unto thee, and lay me down
Upon thy cool, true breast, and let me die!
And now I come, and but one touch of thine
Sends healing through my weary frame once more.
I lean my head on thy unchanging breast,
And draw fresh strength through every vein, and life
In every pore. And all the murmur of
Thy sounding pines, thy trembling, sighing leaves,
Thrills every nerve with sudden joy. Thy breath
Steals soft o'er cheek, and brow, and lip, so full
Of fragrance, bringing back my childhood's days,
That I forget the weary midnight past,
And dream I am a child again. Thy voice,
Thy touch, thy power win back to life once more.
I shall not die.

Teach me, sublime old mount,
To stand like thee, defying clouds and storms,
And wrap the snow-white mantle of a calm
And holy resignation round my soul,
When sorrow's dreary winter-time shall come!
And when 'tis past, like thee reclothe myself
In life's fresh verdure, till the hour shall come
To be reclothed in Higher Worlds, in robes
That young immortals wear, to lose their light
No more forever.

PLYMOUTH, May 24, 1862.

EARLY POEMS.

EARLY POEMS.

THE DYING WARRIOR.*

His gallant form is lying on
The cold and blood-stained ground,
While thunders of the battle-field
Are raging loud around.
His helmet with its waving plume
Is lying by his side,
And from his heart the warm life-blood
Is flowing like a tide.

His blood-stained sword that's been his friend
In many a well-fought field,
Has fallen from his nerveless hand,
Unable now to wield.
The hue of death is on his cheek,
And in his bloodshot eye,
He feels the death-chill on his brow,
And knows that he must die.

"Oh, raise my languid form," he says,
"And let me see once more
The charge of my own legions brave,
As on the foe they pour.

* Mostly composed during sickness.

Go, go to them, and tell them
'Tis my last request, my all,
To onward press to victory,
And avenge their leader's fall!"

They raised him from the cold, damp ground,—
His faithful followers there,—
And wiped the clotted blood from out
His dark and matted hair.
He glanced one moment on the fight—
The spirit fires him now—
"Oh, give me once my steed," he says,
"My helmet on my brow,

"And I will lead my men once more
To victory, or to death!"—
That moment with his life-blood passed
His last, his latest breath.
But victory crowned his banners bright,
His last high wish was granted,
That wish for which his blood was spilt,
For which his soul had panted.

THE WANDERER'S RETURN.

To the wanderer give one welcome
Back, back to his sunny home;
For far away 'mong strangers,
Long, long has been his roam.

He has missed the pleasant fireside,
  The happy household band,
And now he comes once more beneath
  His father's roof to stand.

He comes, his heart grown weary
  With wand'ring far away,
With trials that beset him
  Upon his toilsome way.
He comes once more to visit
  His early boyhood's home,
And once again to listen
  To soft affection's tone.

But where are they — the loved ones,
  For which his spirit craves?
Oh, some are scattered far away,
  And some sleep in their graves.
No mother's voice shall greet him,
  No sister's tender tone,
The green grass waves above them,
  And he is all alone.

He seeks his home in childhood,
  Which once was full of glee,
Where he had knelt in guileless prayer,
  Low at his mother's knee.
But gloomy and deserted
  Are those decaying walls,
And silent are its places, —
  Alas! the lonely halls.

The silent room he enters,
  But all is sadly lone;
No face familiar greets him,
  No joyous, ringing tone.
The echo of his footsteps
  Alone the silence breaks,
Save when the sighing breezes
  A mournful requiem makes.

His shadow on the hearthstone
  Is all that's resting there,—
Ah, no! there's one still deeper,
  'Tis gloomy, dark despair.
Gone is the sound of laughter,
  Of happy, careless mirth,
He stands in silent anguish
  Upon the lonely hearth.

A withering blight comes o'er him,
  He feels that he is now,
"Upon the old ancestral tree
  The last leaf on the bough."
Well might he say, heart-broken,
  In sorrow's deepest tone,
"The hearth, the hearth is desolate,
  The bright fire quenched and gone.

THE DAYS OF OLD.

Oh, the days of Old, the bright days of Old!
I love the tales that about them are told:
I could sit for hours o'er the author's page,
Where are spread bright gems of the by-gone age;—

Of the time when the Normans crossed the main,
O'er the English Isles in their might to reign,
When the Saxons bold held the regal sway,
Till, pressed by hosts, they were forced to give way.

Again, of the knights in the days of old,
With their armor bright and their chargers bold,
Who fought for their homes on many a day,
Or tried their lance in the tourney gay;

Or when, with their zeal in the Holy War,
They went from their homes to a country far,
To fight for their faith and the Holy Land,
In a noble, brave, and warlike band.

How I love to read of bold Robin Hood,
Who dwelt in the shade of merry Sherwood,
With his outlaw band dressed in Lincoln Green,
With their arrows sharp and their hardy mien.

There they lay in wait as the traveller passed,
And summoned their train with the bugle's blast,
Or feasted and sung in their mirth and ease,
'Neath the green, hanging boughs of the forest trees.

And the tales of Greece, in its ancient times,
And the men that peopled its sunny climes
In its infant state, or its lofty height,
In its feeble strength, and its towering might.

There's many a deed of the Spartan told,
Of the fearless soldier and matron bold,
Ere the nation wasted its life in ease,
In the reign of luxurious Pericles.

There's many a hero whose cherished name
Shall be in all ages a wreath of fame ;
There's many a poet whose song divine,
Shall be echoed fore'er from clime to clime,

That once lived in Greece in its palmy day,
When o'er arts and science it held the sway,
Ere the hand of Time had its ruin hurled
O'er the haughty pride of the Grecian world.

And Italy ! over that sunny clime
Strong spells are cast by the olden time,
From Venetian isles to Rome's high towers,
Through her hills and vales, and her myrtle bowers.

And now, though her greatness has passed away,
And Rome, its proud mistress, in ruin lay,
The fame of her sons burns bright in song,
Their names are immortal in virtue or wrong.

And over all lands is a romance cast
By the deeds and words of times long past ;
From the Nile's proud flood to old Scotia's height,
And our own broad Land has its deeds of might.

DARK HOURS.

I'm weary of this dull, cold earth,
  So full of pain and woe;—
Nought save a dreary weight of care
  Ere greets me as I go.

My path grows dark on every side;
  No ray of light is there,
Save Hope's pale glimmering light that scarce
  Can save me from despair.

Along the daily path of some,
  The gifts of Fortune free
Lie scattered, like the pearly dew
  On blossom, leaf, and tree.

But mine winds through a tangled way,
  A dark and dreary wild,
Of hope deferred, of sickening cares,
  Where fortune never smiles.

I may not join the festive mirth
  Of the bright and joyous throng,
Where beauty, wit, and gladness, reign,
  And the magic tone of song.

I may not range the valleys wide
  To cull the fairest flowers,
Or while some leisure hour away
  Beneath the forest bowers.

I may not climb the rocky steep,
At twilight's hour so still,
There sit and let wild fancy stray
Far onward at its will.

But I must pass long hours of gloom,
When all around is bright,
For o'er my form Disease has lain
Its withering, sickening blight.

Yet I could bear my dreary lot,
With scarce one murmuring thought,
Might I but drink at Science's fount
A deep, soul-filling draught;

Might I but read the thrilling page
Of ancient, mystic lore,
And learn the many deeds of those
Who lived in days of yore;

Or clothe the bright and glowing thought
With deep and burning words,
That make the heart with rapture thrill
Whene'er the tone is heard.

MUSINGS.

THE sunlight falls across the room,
  This bright and glorious day,
And snowy fields like crystal shine
  Beneath its dazzling ray.
The hanging ice from every tree
  Reflects the rainbow's hue,
The arching vault of heaven has caught
  A deeper, darker blue.

I hear the merry sleigh-bells chime;
  The laugh of passers-by
Falls coldly on my weary ear,
  And dims my aching eye.
I cannot bear the sounds of mirth,
  'Tis mockery in my ears;
And joyous smiles wake bitterness
  That I must quench in tears.

For there's no pulse within my heart
  At joyous tones to thrill,
But throbs of agony instead,
  I vainly try to still.
A crushing weight of misery
  Is on my spirit laid,
And 'neath its shade of bitterness
  Hope's light must darkly fade.

O God! has not my lot from youth
  Been hard enough to bear,
That this last stroke — the worst of all —
  Is added to my share?
Had I not known enough of grief,
  E'en in my happiest hour,
Enough of all the storms that fate
  Upon my head might shower?

From childhood's hour have I not felt
  That life is cold and drear,
With nought to me save bitterness,
  And trouble, doubt, and fear?
Had I not drank of poverty
  Full many a bitter cup,
And often as I drank the dregs
  Again it was filled up?

And now a deeper, darker shade
  Is o'er my spirit cast
By wan disease; that bows my form.
  Oh, is not this the last?
Oh, for a place where I may lay
  My weary, aching head,
Oh, for one hour of peaceful rest,
  E'en though 'twere with the dead!

THE SHIP.

A GALLANT Ship has left the strand, and cleaves the foaming deep,
And onward like a thing of life her course undaunted keeps,
She's freighted with a priceless load of many happy hearts,
And some, filled with wild agony, compelled from friends to part.

There's some upon her deck who love to trust the treacherous tide;
And some, to view Earth's thousand scenes, her hills and valleys wide,
To gaze upon her far-famed towers, her high and lofty domes,
And feast the mind with lovely things, have left their sunny homes.

And some, long exiles from their homes in their loved native land,
Till every lock is silvered o'er by Time's relentless hand,
Turn once again to view the hills and plains of that dear spot
That through their wanderings o'er the earth has never been forgot.

And some, to win the flush of health back to their pallid cheek,
Have bade their homes and friends farewell with anguish none might speak ;
For who could tell if those loved forms might fill a lonely grave,
Or, far more sad than aught beside, be buried 'neath the wave !

Ah, who can tell the anxious eyes that watch them from the shore,
Or know the dark forebodings sad that they should meet no more,
Or guess each throb of anguish wild when lowering tempests rise,
And howling winds with dirge-like blast sweep through the darkening skies ?

The sky is calm, the breezes light, the Ship speeds o'er the main,
Bearing her load of human hearts, — will she return again ?
Though now awhile the sky is fair, and wind and tempests sleep,
They, e'er to-morrow's dawn, may rise, and shroud her in the deep.

And all the wealth of joyous hearts that with high rapture beat,
To view once more their native land, and friends and kindred meet,

May all be hushed and coldly still beneath the dashing
wave,
Where none may know their lonely bed, or weep above
their grave.

The friends who loved them fondly well, may never
know their fate,
But by their fireside lone and sad through long dark
hours may wait,
To greet the loved one's form once more, the well
known voice to hear,
To welcome their return with smiles, long hoped with
prayers and tears.

A VOICE FROM FRANCE, 1848.

THERE'S a rushing sound like a mighty wind
In Paris' crowded street,
There's a murmur like the ocean's roar,
And the sound of many feet.

Down, down with the King! bursts forth from the
throng;
Let him mingle in the dust;
From the princely halls of the Tuileries
Let the throne be rudely thrust!

Let the symbols dark of a king's proud reign,
No more be seen in our land;
Let us rise, and free ourselves from the scourge
Of a tyrant's bloody hand!

Shall we tremble still at a king's stern frown,
And like cowards turn and flee,
When with efforts brave, and a dauntless heart,
We might all as well be free?

Let us raise the flag, the tri-colored flag,
That has oft to victory led,
When our countrymen fought at Napoleon's side,
And their blood was freely shed.

And teach the broad world that we will be free,
That the victory shall be ours;
Although no Napoleon wins the fight,
We've a brighter, better power.

For the God of truth and liberty now
Will guide us on by his might,
Till the land shall hold no slave to base power,
But all have a freeman's right.

Then let us arise, and burst the chains
That were forged by a tyrant's hand;
Let us plant the Tree of Liberty now,
That forevermore shall stand.

THOUGHTS ON LEAVING HOME.

Must I now leave thee, thou home
Of my childhood's mirth?
Must I bid a farewell
To my father's hearth?

Must I leave all the friends
That I've treasured here,
And the beautiful scenes
That to me are dear?

Yes, yes, I must leave ye,—
Each bright sunny glade,
Each beautiful prospect
In sunlight and shade.

I must go from my home
To a stranger land,
I must sever the chord
Of the household band.

I shall then no more know
A mother's fond prayer,
The love of a sister,
Or a brother's care.

In the home of a stranger
My lot is now cast;—
Is it strange that I grieve
For joys that are past?

The grief of a moment
  Is passing away,
For much as I love home,
  Yet I would not stay.

The far-off world calls me,
  In visions so bright,
When imagination
  Takes its far flight, —

That I must e'en leave thee,
  In strange lands to dwell:
So all that I love here,
  Farewell! farewell!

THE MOURNER.

The birds are singing sweetly
  Upon the maple bough;
The fragrant breath of summer
  Is floating round me now.

The earth is decked with flowers,
  The groves are green and bright;
These old familiar places
  Are filled with joy and light.

But all to me is darkness,
  To me is filled with gloom;
For the loved, the loved are sleeping,
  Cold in the silent tomb.

The birds' glad song but mocks me;
  I cannot bear the tone;
Amid this mirth and gladness
  I feel alone, *alone*.

The world is dark and dreary,
  To me its light is fled;
And every sight and sound to me
  Speaks only of the dead.

DISEASE.

I SIT me down with troubled thoughts and wildly aching head,
I'm lonely, sad, dispirited, hope seems forever fled;
My mind is all one chaos dark of visions wild and strange,
That one by one with startling force before me seem to range.
The hand of grief with leaden weight is pressing on my brow,
And 'neath its weight of heaviness my stricken form must bow;

All things that meet my saddened gaze a gloomy aspect wear,
And life a weary, weary way, almost too hard to bear.

Earth's false, deceitful charms that shone in fancy's mirror bright,
Are withered now, and seem but dust and ashes in my sight;
Joys faded pass in long array before my spirit's eye,
And fain I'd seek some lonely place, and lay me down and die.
Why am I left to drag out life in woe, and care, and pain,
Bewailing hours of happiness that ne'er may come again;
Still grieving for the health once mine, so early, sadly lost;
My youthful days chilled with disease's cold, withering, blighting blast?

And must I ever thus remain, must I thus linger so,
Through long, long years (perhaps through life), with all this weight of woe?
Oh, must I move in sadness 'mid the busy, bustling throng,
And feel my weakness every hour when I would fain be strong?
My soul is struggling hard within its earthly prison-cell,
And burning thoughts that none may speak with wildest passion swell;

And now I feel the chords that bind my spirit to this
clay,
And chain its freedom, when it fain would rise and
soar away.

What's left me now but agony and soul-subduing grief?
Which way I turn, where'er I look, nought gives my
soul relief;
I still must linger on through life, in weariness and
woe,
A stranger to the joys of health, a prisoner here below.
But hush, my heart, thy wild regrets! thy vain repin-
ing still!
And learn to bow thyself beneath a higher, holier Will;
Arouse thy better thoughts that long beneath despair
have slept,
And burst the bonds that bind thee back to joys so
wildly wept.

Learn to endure thy bitter lot without one murmuring
sigh,
Learn to submit to One All-Wise who rules both earth
and sky,
Who giveth, in his mercy, joy and grief to all beneath
the sun,
Who doeth all things well, and guides and guards each
suffering one.
I will arise, and cast aside the dark and burning
thoughts,
With which my fevered brain has been so wildly, mad-
ly fraught,

And nerve my spirit up to meet the worst that life can
give,
To calmly bear my weary lot with firmness while I live.

TO A BUNCH OF VIOLETS IN MY SICK ROOM.

Bright flowers of the Spring-time!
I see ye once more,
With thy beauty as peerless
As ever before.

O'er the reign of stern Winter
Bright Spring has the sway,
She has broken the ice-chains
That bound thee, away.

And my heart feels more joyful
To gaze on thee now,
Though the hand of pale sickness
Is laid on my brow.

Oh, I cannot but love thee,
Bright, beautiful flowers!
For thou bring'st me bright visions
Of sweet, sunny hours; —

Of the hours when I rambled
  Among the green bowers,
Where thy blossoms lay hidden
  By green leaves and flowers.

Oh, ye seem like an old friend,
  In beauty and power,
That clings only closer
  In sorrow's dark hour!

THEY BID ME NERVE MY DROOPING SOUL.

They bid me nerve my drooping soul
  To bear my weary lot,
As though the ills of life could be
  So easily forgot.

They bid me turn my weary eyes
  Life's brightest side to see;
As if the rays thus cast on some,
  Would ever beam on me.

They tell me brighter days will come,
  That Health will yet be mine;
They bid me still my aching thoughts,
  And cease thus to repine.

As though 'twere not a harder task
To still my throbbing heart,
Than 'tis for them to coldly say.,
"Bear well thy bitter part."

As if I e'er could fondly hope
My lost health to regain,
When I have wished and fondly hoped
For years, and found it vain.

I could have borne a father's fall
From honor, truth, and fame,
And heard the word of *drunkard* placed
With his once honored name;

Although it is enough, methinks,
The stoutest heart to break,
And from the path of life around
The brightest flowers to shake;

And Poverty's cold, chilling blast
Unshrinking I could bear,
Although the world turns coldly from
The child of want and care;

But when to these unnumbered ills
Is added wan Disease,
That palsies all the warm life-blood,
And bids the current cease,

Then hope casts but a sick'ning ray
  To guide me as I go,
And life seems filled with naught to me,
  Save pain and want and woe ; —

To watch the long, long weary days
  Drag slowly, sadly by,
And know that each returning sun
  Will rise in majesty,

And mock me with its gorgeous rays
  When I am filled with gloom,
And shed its beams in mockery
  Within my darkened room ;

To hear the birds with joyous tone
  Pour forth their gladsome song,
And upward wing their flight in air,
  So joyous all day long ;

And feel the yearning in my soul
  To be as free as they,
And know my hopes are fettered by
  This feeble, dying clay.

I cannot hush the throbbing wild
  That swells through every vein,
When memory points to happy days
  That ne'er may come again.

They think that I can cast aside
  Such vain and wild regrets,
Perhaps I ought,—yet how can I,
  With such a dreary lot?

SING TO ME.

Sing to me some strain enlivening,
  For I am sad to-night!
Oh, sing me something seeming
  To speak of hope and light!

For feelings strange and withering
  Have o'er my spirit fell,
And Memory stern is working
  Its dark and fearful spell.

Oh, thousand thoughts of sadness
  Are stealing through my mind,
And round my crowded vision
  Their darksome fibres wind.

I think of earth's false pleasures,
  And all its bitter woe,
Till my mind is past controlling,
  And I almost wish to go

"Where the wicked cease from troubling,
And the weary are at rest;"
In that home that is appointed,
With all the good and blest.

Then sing me something cheering;
And I will try to cast
Aside the bitter feelings
Of the dark and gloomy Past.

TO MY SISTER ON HER EIGHTEENTH BIRTHDAY.

SISTER, our life is but a dream,
And we are hastening down the stream
That glides so fast;
Just eighteen years have passed away
Since thou beheld the light of day,—
How soon it past!

How short the time now seems to me
Since we sat down beneath the trees,
Beneath the shade;
Or sported on the grass so green,
Or through the fields with joyous mien,
We gaily strayed.

When we would cull the fairest flowers
That grew among the mossy bowers,
    In early spring;
And list to hear the wild bird's song,
As through the air it swept along,
    A joyous thing.

And when the summer came at last,
And all the berries ripened fast
    Beneath the sun:
Then, with our baskets in our hand,
To gather them, — a happy band, —
    We swiftly run.

And when we'd picked a goodly share
Of all that were most nice and fair,
    We never stayed;
But hastened home with longing eye,
To gaze upon the strawberry-pie
    That mother made.

I well remember how we dressed
Our dolls up in their very best,
    To make them show;
And William then would plague and tease,
And never give us any ease,
    Or peace, you know.

And when we must to school away,
We almost wished at home to stay,
    To tend them well;

But when once there, we soon forgot
Their wants, in learning in that spot,
To read and spell.

And when the winter came with snow
And ice, — when all the boys could go,
And slide so smart;
While you stood back with timid fear,
I always thought the "coast was clear,"
And took a part.

And then, sometimes, we'd have a slide
Upon the sled that swiftly glides
Adown the hill;
With girls and boys in merry play,
When we could ever steal away
'Gainst mother's will.

But childhood's hours have passed away,
And with them all our merry play,
And dreams of bliss;
For after years bring pain and care,
And we must learn such things to bear
In a world like this.

This life at best is full of woe,
As all who live too soon must know,
With bitter fears;
For all our hopes are but as dust,
And all their sweetest visions must
Be quenched in tears.

For Hope smiles only to deceive;
And yet we still that smile believe
When all is fair;
But when affliction's hour draws nigh,
Our happy thoughts are fettered by
A dark despair.

I think we both so soon have quaffed
From life's full cup a bitter draught
Of pain and care;
And yet perhaps 'tis but a drop
Compared to all within the cup,
To be our share.

Yet sometimes 'mid the gathering night,
There gushes forth a ray of light
To guide our way;
That makes all things in gladness bloom,
Once shrouded by the darkest gloom,
And bids us stay.

And earth seems then a region blest,
Where many souls may seek for rest,
And find at last.
But ah, 'tis but a sunbeam stray
That through the clouds had found its way;—
It soon is past.

'Tis thus that life appears to me,
Yet brighter it may seem to thee
Than to my eyes;

May such glad feelings never fade,
And may no deeper, darker shade
E'er dim thy skies.

And thou hast passed from childhood now,
For eighteen years have swept thy brow
With flying wing;
And thou must bear life's hopes and fears,
For in thy heart are *woman's tears*, —
A hidden spring.

Let not the fount be lightly stirred
By winning smiles, and love's soft words
In tender tone;
"Who learns to love, but learns to weep,
And tearful, nightly vigils keep,"
In sorrow lone.

Shun dark temptation's devious way,
Encompassed round by fancy's gay
And treacherous net;
And let each false, alluring charm,
Spread forth to lure thee on to harm,
Be firmly met.

And if thy heart sometimes will fail,
And shrink beneath the passing gale
That round thee sweeps;
Think of a home beyond the grave,
Of Him who will thy spirit save,
And ever keep.

LAMENT OF THE JEWISH CAPTIVES.

By Babylon's lone river, far in a stranger's land,
Were gathered all together our sad and broken band;
And there with hearts fast breaking, while all around us slept,
Upon their banks by moonlight we sat us down and wept.
We wept for Zion fallen from all her greatness now,
While we poor, lonely captives to servitude must bow;
We wept to think how strangers now dwelt within her walls,
And held their mirth and pastime in our deserted halls.

We wept, and oh! how vainly, to think we never there,
Within our holy temple, might meet again in prayer,
Where we had met to worship our own and fathers' God,
For now far off we're scattered, beneath his chastening rod.
Our harps upon the willows we had in silence hung,
For now their strings were tuneless, and palsied were our tongues;
And oft the eve's breeze sweeping among the jarring strings,
To our lone ear desponding, a mournful cadence brings.

And they that bound us captive in servitude so long,
With mocking tone and gestures required of us a song,

Saying, "Sing us one of Zion, — the long-remembered
lays,
When ye were met to worship your God with prayer
and praise."
But never to those strangers shall songs like ours be
sung,
No! rather let each harp-string forever be unstrung,
No! rather let the willows their mournful burden
bear, —
Yet still relief is left us — 'tis fervent, heart-felt prayer!

ADDRESS OF HENRY THE FOURTH TO HIS ARMY.

"Soldiers of Navarre and reformed France!" cried he, waving aloft his lance, "do you want a banner to fight under? Then follow my white plume, and turn not your horses' heads till you see it laid in the dust."

Henry Quatre.

YES, on to the rescue, soldiers all!
Nor fear ye the fate of those that fall.
Yes, on to regain your banner proud,
And win ye a name, or find a shroud!

No time is this for a craven heart,
No time to shirk from a soldier's part!
Would a banner cheer your spirits on,
To fight in a cause that *must* be won?

Then behold my plume that is waving high!
Follow this, nor think ye once to fly,
Nor swerve from your post until ye must,
Till this plume and head are laid in dust!

Thus he spake: then plunged in thickest fight,
While his army, now restrained from flight,
With their leader's war-cry hurried on,
To charge the ranks of the foe again.

They followed that plume where the battle raged,
And with hearts of steel the combat waged,
Nor turned their backs till the foe were crushed,
And their banner raised from out the dust.

TO ONE WHO CALLED ME UNGRATEFUL.

I'M not ungrateful, though I seem
To thee so base and weak;
I'm not ungrateful — ne'er again
To me such dark words speak.

Think you that I remember not
The kindness done to me?
Think you I have forgotten all
My gratitude to thee?

What though I seem unheeding all
  The blessings thou dost shower,
To all thy cheering words and deeds
  In dark affliction's hour;

What though my lips speak not the thanks
  That I have owed thee long;
Yet not the less around my heart
  Do grateful feelings throng.

For every kindly word and deed,
  For all thy tender care,
For happiness to thee and thine,
  I breathe a fervent prayer.

A friend in need thou proved to me,
  When storm-clouds swept the sky,
When wan disease was o'er me laid,
  And dark affliction nigh.

For this my heart will thank thee, though
  My lips are silent still,
For this will endless gratitude
  To thee, my spirit fill.

And should you ever think me strange,
  And cold, and most unkind,
Yet deeper still those thoughts shall burn,
  Still deeper in my mind.

And if I never may repay
  The bounties thou hast given,
Yet still rewarded thou shalt be, —
  'Tis treasured up in Heaven!

DESPAIR.

I'LL hope no more; — 'tis all in vain!
For health can ne'er be mine again:
I've hoped and prayed through weary years,
I've craved the boon with bitter tears;
But 'tis in vain, — 'tis all in vain, —
It never can be mine again.

I'll think no more of joyous hours,
No more of life's bright sunny flowers;
For all that made my joy is fled,
And all life's flowers are torn and dead:
I've struggled on through pain and care,
But now I yield to dark Despair.

Yet I had hoped that life would be
A scene of active joy to me, —
I wished to do, to act, to give,
I wished for more than just to live:
It may not be; and I must still
My aching heart to do His will.

And now 'tis past! and I am left
Of all life's brightest joys bereft;
My spirit crushed, that fain would rise
With eagle pinion to the skies.
The world is dark! to hope were vain,
For health can ne'er be mine again.

"SUFFER, YET BE STRONG."

Yes, suffer if thou must! but oh, be strong,
Although thy trials may be stern and long,
And filled with sorrows dark, that make the heart
Almost too sad to bear its bitter part.
What though thy path is Poverty's lone way
Uncheered by naught save hope's pale, dying ray?
Yet let thy heart be strong; press on in might;—
Bright days will come, if thou but doest right.

Has wan Disease her blight upon thee laid,
And caused the bright light from thine eye to fade?
Does health with taunting mien thy sad prayers spurn,
Still mocking with a vain hope of return?
Yet still hope on; despair not even then;
For time may bring thee back thy strength again;
And patient suffering through the weary hours,
May give thy soul far better thoughts and powers.

Have friends turned coldly from thy path aside,—
Those whom thou ever thought the true, the tried,—

And left thee in affliction's stern, cold hour,
To meet alone the dark storm-clouds that lower?
Let not thy heart be sad for friends so frail,
But nerve *thyself* to meet the passing gale;
Bow thy form meekly 'neath the chastening rod,
And learn to put thy trust in none but God.

Have those whose presence rendered bright thy way —
Too pure, too meek, in this cold world to stay —
Been called from earth, the chain of bondage riven?
Grieve not, but think thou'lt meet them all in Heaven;
And know that round thee still the loved ones come,
To render bright the darkness of thy home.
Yes, God's own love is round thee every hour;
Lean strong and fearless on His mighty power!

RECOVERY FROM SICKNESS.

My heart was almost breaking
  In those dark hours of pain,
But now once more I'm waking
  To light and hope again.

The hours were dark and lonely
  Until thou came at last;
But now I know I only
  Should thank thee for the past.

Oh, when I lay enshrouded
  In darkness and despair,
And hope's bright star was clouded,
  Then thou wert with me there.

But ah, amid my anguish,
  I knew not thou wert nigh;
My doom was then to languish,
  Methought alone to die.

But glorious light is breaking
  Within my prison's gloom,
And now new flowers are waking—
  New flowers of fadeless bloom.

To thee, O God, I'm raising
  An anthem glad and free,
And every hour I'm praising,
  O God, I'm praising Thee!

"ONLY FOR ONE."

SUGGESTED BY THE REMARK OF A FRIEND.

At times my soul beneath the power
  Of some strange spell is stirred,
As though an Angel sang to me,
  And I that song had heard;

As though some power within my soul
  Burst forth like morning sun,
And thrilled to music every chord —
  I only sing for one.

And sometimes, when my spirit-lyre
  Is swept in every string,
And glows with inspiration's fire,
  As touched by angel's wing,
I fain would paint in glowing verse,
  As others oft have done,
And give expression to my thought,
  Yet only write for one.

I gaze far down the aisles of life,
  As in some chapel dim,
And note the pilgrim's morning prayer,
  Or list his evening hymn;
And whether in the morning hour,
  Or when the day is done,
I watch the passers come and go,
  Yet only look for one.

Yet through that one, as through a glass,
  The world I seem to see,
And like an image stands that one
  Of all the world to me;
And through that inspiration given,
  As through some morning sun,
I sing, and write, and act for all,
  Best when it *seems* for one.

LINES WRITTEN IN A SCHOOL-ROOM.

THE school-room is deserted now,
The happy children gone,
And silence rests upon the spot
So strangely, sadly lone.

There's loneliness within the walls;
I miss the little feet
That echoed here a moment since,
And filled each vacant seat.

Gone is each voice of happiness,
And childhood's joyous tone,
And with my sad and lonely thoughts
Once more I'm left alone.

But now, methinks, the air seems filled
With spirits of the past,—
A strange, sweet spell is in the air,
And all around me cast.

The echoes of the youthful tones
That rung here long ago,
Steal o'er me like the far-off strain
Of music soft and low.

A fairy throng steal softly back
To their accustomed place,
And every vacant seat is filled
With an unfamiliar face.

A bright and joyous band are they;
  The same sweet smile is there,
That often when within these walls
  Their features used to wear.

And with them back they bring the light
  Of childhood's happy days,
And round the room that lonely seemed
  They shed sweet, brightening rays.

And o'er my soul the influence falls
  Like some soft ray of light,—
All loneliness and gloom is past,
  All, all around seems bright.

SONGS FROM SPIRIT LAND.

I.

Melody, melody! list and ye'll hear!
Angels are singing; the loved ones are near!
Harmony, harmony! songs of pure love
Are floating to greet thee from Bright Ones above!

Can ye not hear it? Then listen again!
'Twould fill thee with rapture to catch the glad strain.
Anthems, glad anthems, are rising to God;
Join in those anthems, O loved, on this sod!

Sweeter and sweeter that strain still shall grow,
When mortals shall join us, — the loved ones below;
Louder, still louder our paeans shall be,
When Earth from her darkness shall rise and be free!

II.

Burst forth in a song of praise,
O Earth! to God, your King;
The deepest tribute of your hearts
To Him forever bring.

He formed the earth, the sea, the air,
He formed the spreading sky,
And every star that nightly comes
To cheer the gazing eye.

And every little flower that grows
In wild or desert place,
Is but the index of His smile,
A symbol of His grace.

Time was when earth was not, or stars,
Or planetary world,
Or suns, or systems; nought but God
Wide through all space unfurled.

He spake; and worlds on worlds came forth,
And took the place designed,
And each is held in measured course
By His directing mind.

MORNING.

SEE! Aurora's crimson beam
  Wakes to lighten all the world:
See each tint in beauty gleam;
  From his throne grim Night is hurled!

Now the sun with crown of light
  Ushers in the glorious Day;
Clouds that hid the face of night,
  Gleam like gold beneath his ray.

Thus may Knowledge ever be
  Round our minds a halo bright;
Thus may we, delighted, see
  Wisdom's rays disperse the night.

THE ANGEL'S VISIT.

November winds were loud and high,
The storm-clouds drifted through the sky,
And, hid behind a frowning pile,
The sun refused for man to smile.
The earth had lost its sylvan sheen,
The forest trees their robes of green,
And tossed their naked branches high,
As if for succor to the sky,
In this their bitter trial day,—
Their all of beauty passed away.
The giant mountains, late so green,
Like rocky ramparts now were seen,
And frowning down upon the vale,
Seemed adding terror to the gale;
And over all, the murky clouds
Closed, dark and gloomy like a shroud.
And that strange, deep and mystic sound
Which Autumn breathes through all around,—
Her own sad dirge upon the day
When all her children pass away,—
Seemed strangely sad in that dark hour;
Now bursting forth with frenzied power,
As if the smothered grief of years,
Welled out in groans, and prayers, and tears;

'Twas now a fitful, gasping sigh,
Like one who struggled, but must die;
And now a wild, unearthly groan,
Like some poor sufferer's dying moan;
Then soft and low, a plaintive strain,
That thrilled the heart with sudden pain,
That told of suffering and of care,
Of blighted hopes, of dark despair.
So dark, so eerie was the tone,
The heart grew desolate and lone.

Within a vale where mountains high
Stood up as pillars for the sky,
And autumn's dirge went wailing on,
As though it murmured, "Gone, all gone,"
A young girl lay in darkened room,
Chained by disease, — a living tomb!
And what to her was cloud or sky?
Such sights might never greet *her* eye.
And what was coming day or night?
To her, alas, there was *no light!*
What to her was Spring's bright morn?
She could not see its flowery dawn.
And what were Summer's glorious rays,
Its long, its bright, sunshiny days?
Could Autumn's dirge e'er give her pain?
Sang not *her* heart a *sadder* strain?
And cheek and lip, and heart and eye,
Gave but this prayer — "*Oh, God, to die!*"
And wonder not she breathed such prayer,
And wonder not at her despair;

For, long and weary years she'd lain
Upon her couch of torturing pain ;
Such years as make the heart grow old,
The fires of life burn dim and cold ;
Such years as hush young life's rich thrill,
And *crush* the heart, or make it still.
There *was* a time when, glad and gay,
She speeded on her earthly way,
And though the clouds were round her path,
She heeded not their stormy wrath,
But still hoped on, *one wish to gain*,—
Alas, alas, how wholly vain !
She cared not for the wealth of worlds,
For Fame's broad banner wide unfurled ;
But there was thirst her soul within,
The fount of Science, Truth, to win.
She heard far off the dashing waves
That this bright shrine forever lave ;
She prayed the voices of the past
Their mystic light for her to cast ;
She asked to feed the mind with lore,
Such as the ancients had in store ;
For Genius, Intellect, and Power,
To be her bright, immortal dower ;
To wander on as hand in hand
With gifted minds, a radiant band.
But that deep thirst might not be still,
There came no power her soul to fill ;
She only caught the dashing spray
Of those bright waters far away,
That only bathed her parching lip —
The chaliced cup she might not sip.

Then came Disease with withering spell,
And o'er her hopes its dark blight fell,
And o'er her form; and there she lay
A suffering captive, day by day;
The same deep thirst within her soul,
Whose maddened waves but wilder rolled.
And there, as year by year passed on,
Without one hope to lean upon,
No voice to say, thou shalt again
Come forth among the haunts of men,
(For e'en the skilful could not cope,
But whispered low, "There is no hope,")
Her memory faded like a dream,
From out the world, with passing gleam.
She learned to know the weary lot
Of those who live to be forgot;
Or but remembered still as one
From whom the love of life had gone;
Who turned her face unto the wall,
And listened only for her call;
Who bowed her head to meet her fate,
And waited lonely at the Gate.

What knew they of her wild despair?
What knew they of her ceaseless prayer?
Of all her struggles, still to gain
Her health, her place in life again,
That she might yet drink at the spring,
Whose thrilling waves such rapture bring?
That she might live, *not all in vain*,
But for the world some lasting gain.

And then, when came the crushing blow,
That she must still live on in woe,
That health might never come again,
That she must live, ay, *worse* than vain,
To make no human pathway bright,
But with her *shadow* cast a blight;
And that for every breath she drew,
A *mother's* heart must bleed anew,
And every comfort that might cheer,
Was purchased by a mother's tear,
And all her life was adding now
But wrinkles to that mother's brow;
How prayed her heart still o'er and o'er,
With agony unfelt before,
Until, with every labored breath,
Came welling forth, "Where art thou, Death?"
Thou comest to the glad and gay,
Thou bearest them from earth away,
And thou dost lay the mighty low,
Till nations wail in bitter woe;
And yet thou passest coldly by,
When all my prayer is, *Let me die!*
And am I then so *slight* a thing,
Thou deem'st me not worth conquering;
In pain and grief am I so low,
Thou *scorn'st* to be to *such* a foe?
Or dost thou laugh at my despair,
Exulting in my fruitless prayer,
And, feeling that the hell I live
Is greater than *thy power* can give,
So leavest me, with a torturer's art,
To suffer on with breaking heart,

To triumph in thy fiendish glee,
My tortured agony to see;
And coldly pass, in this my hour
Of bitterest need of all thy power,—
To leave me with my Cross of Fire,
With every flame but rising higher,
Upon the rack extended now,
The Crown of Thorns upon my brow,—
To aim thy dart where shrieks of fear
Shall sound when'er thy step draws near,
And wails of grief, and tears must flow,
And mankind curse thee in their woe?

"O Death! thou tyrant, hated thing!
Thou art the conqueror of Kings.
The maiden's cheek grows pale with fear,
When thou dost whisper, 'I am here!'
The lover's heart that wildly thrills,
At touch of thine grows strangely still;
The *victor* of the conquering fight,
Is but the *victim* of *thy* might;
And warriors brave that dare thy spell,
Leave but this story—'Here they fell.'
No wonder all the world's thy foe,
For thou hast laid their *great ones* low;
No wonder that they shrink in dread
Upon thy breast to lean their head!
Cold-hearted one! thou wilt not tell
Where thou hast taken the loved to dwell,
Whether to Heaven, or yet to Hell;
Or whether thou leav'st them in the grave,
To slumber in oblivion's wave

Forever. None but those who lie
In *Earth's* deep Hell, can pray to die!"—
Such was *her* fate. Thou wouldst not come
To take her to thy mystic home.
A greater tyrant reigned o'er her —
Thou *wouldst* not be its conqueror;
A darker fate than *thou* canst give;
Thy fiendish heart said, "Let her live!"

And in this hour of Autumn's gloom,
When earth was shrouding for the tomb,
And dirge-like music swept the blast,
As mourning over blessings past,
She lay in deep and cold despair,
Too deep for tears, too dark for prayer.
And hour by hour dragged slowly by,
And still she lifted not her eye;
The storm grew loud, the thunders rolled,
It waked no echo in her soul;
Cold, silent, prayerless in her gloom,
Like corse just shrouded for the tomb.
And then, as if some mighty spell
Had touched her heart, a wondrous swell
Of wild, impassioned, burning prayer
Burst forth upon the midnight air;
A prayer in which the blight of years,
The bitter, burning, scalding tears,
The blasted hopes, the burning thirst,
Despair — when fate had done its worst, —
All mingled, in heart-breaking wail
More dirge-like than the passing gale;

And in its power went up to God,
Through paths that once the Angels trod:
"O, Mighty Father of us all,
Canst thou not hear me when I call?
Have I not prayed in agony,
Through weary years, O God, to Thee,
For life, for health, for strength once more,
And *e'en for Death*, from out thy store?
Have I not vowed my life should be
A consecration unto Thee?
That where Thy voice might call, I'd go,
O'er land or sea, through weal or woe?
A martyr unto Truth I'd be,
If Thou wouldst set thy captive free,
And let me live an *active* life,
E'en though through want, and woe, and strife?
Vain have I lived, ay, *worse* than vain!
Why art Thou mute, Great God, again?
Are there no Angels now in Heaven,
That unto man are ever given
To comfort, when the soul must weep
Such "tears of blood," and vigils keep
"Within the garden" of the soul,
Where midnight thunders awful roll?
And are there none to "roll away
The stone" from sepulchres to-day?
No angels bright amid this gloom,
To enter now my living tomb,
And touch my form, and bid me rise,
And make this earth a paradise?
From *living death* to set me free,—
A "Resurrection" unto Thee?

If such a boon thou e'er dost give,
Look on me, pity, let me live!
No more with every heart-string riven;
Oh, give to me as thou *hast* given!
Deny me not, mysterious Heaven!

Was it the rush of angels' wings?
Was it the song that seraphs sing?
For scarce had died that anguished prayer
Upon the darkened midnight air,
When, soft and low, a sweet refrain
Gave back the words, again, again,
As if some presence filled the spot,
"*Deny me not, deny me not!*"
A glorious light filled all the place,
Its radiance shone o'er all her face,
Gone, gone, was all her pall-like gloom,
As if bright angels filled the room.
A spell stole through her inmost soul,
She felt its waves in beauty roll;
Gone, gone, was all her pain and care,
She felt no thirst and no despair;
And strength through all her form was given —
"Was she transported unto heaven?
Or had bright angels come to earth,
To raise her to a higher birth?"
As if in answer to this thought,
In melody these words she caught, —
Like angel voices through the room, —
"*God heard thy prayer, we come, we come!*"

A wild, wild thought swept o'er her then,
That she should wake to life again,
That her deep prayers were heard in Heaven,
That angels unto her were given,
To cast away her veil of gloom,
To lift her from her living tomb.
With one wild burst of sudden tears,—
Like rain from heaven o'er all *those years*,—
Her soul gushed forth in living love,
In gratitude to Heaven above.
Like rock when smitten by the rod,
Was that young soul, when touched by God.
And from that hour new strength was given
By those bright messengers from Heaven.
The life-blood, with a sudden start,
Once more pulsated through the heart,
And waked new life in every vein,
Till that poor form revived again.
Until, as day by day passed on,
And week by week sped swiftly on,
That maiden left her couch of pain,
And stepped forth into life again.
Again the sunshine met her eye,
And those Green Mountains, grand and high;
Again she saw the forest trees
Wave green and fragrant in the breeze;
Again beheld earth's carpet bright,
As if just spread to meet her sight,
All woven with its brightest flowers;
She heard the birds amid the bowers,
That seemed to sing their sweetest strain,
As if to welcome back again

One who had loved their woodland song,
And pined to hear it, *oh, so long!*
And how felt she? Like captive freed
In some dark hour of sorest need.
She gazed upon the sunny sky,
She watched the streamlet flowing by,
She wandered in the greenwood shade,
And rested in the shadowy glade;
Drank in the sunshine and the breeze,
And rested 'neath the tall green trees,
With such a gush of grateful love
To that Great Father, God above,
As bade her half forget her pain,
And make her "love to live" again.
And round her still, in every hour,
Was this same bright, angelic power
(That woke her from her pain and woe),
Attending still where she might go.
It came in balmy sleep at night,
At morning's hour it woke to light;
Was with her in the woodland bower,
Gave brighter hues to every flower;
The living presence ever nigh,
Charmed earth and sea, and air and sky,
Till every place her footsteps trod
Seemed hallowed with the Present God.

And stronger grew her form each day,—
All pain and languor swept away,—
Until, like some neglected lute,
With broken strings all sadly mute,

That some kind hand has tuned again,
And waked to old, familiar strain,
Her heart vibrated; and each string
Seemed swept by angels' starry wings,
And gave forth songs whose every tone
Was waked by angel hands alone.
She spoke such words of heavenly truth
And life, as fitted not her youth;
And taught of angels, God and Heaven,
And said that not one tie was riven
When loved ones, called away from earth,
Awoke in Heaven to purer birth.
But that they came again in love,
To point the weary heart above,
To heal the sick, to turn from sin,
To nobler truths the soul to win,
To save from pain, and woe, and care,
To lift above all dark despair,
To wipe away the mourner's tear,
And unto *all* to speak of cheer,
To light with hope each weary eye,
And teach the soul it cannot die.

Enrapt, like one inspired of old,
Forth from her lips such teachings rolled,
Till lost to self the voice would say,
"'Tis Angels speak to you to-day.
This form has languished long in pain,
But we have given it life again;
And we will work for suffering earth,
And wake new flowers of life to birth,

Till all shall know that our bright band
With human souls walks hand in hand." —
And mankind listened when she spoke,
While light o'er all her features broke,
And marvelled much. "What is the power,"
They argued, "that in this dark hour
Has brought her from her living tomb,
Waked unto life, with sudden bloom?
And what has wreathed her face in light?
And what has given her voice such might?
Why do the words like torrents flow,
And speak of Heaven to all below?
Why leaves she woman's lowly sphere,
To speak where crowds these words can hear,
When all the men of God but say,
She doth blaspheme, — away, away?
And thoughtless worldlings scorn to hear
A message from the brighter sphere,
Or say our friends in heaven are blest;
Call them not back, but let them rest!
"'Tis strange, 'tis passing strange," they say, —
"By ignis fatuus led away!
What spell is woven o'er her brain?
And yet what power assuaged her pain?"
And some looked, listened, and believed,
Rejoicing in the truth received;
And many a mourner wiped the tear,
The loved one's voice from heaven to hear.
And many a suffering form of pain,
Arose to life and light again;
And many an erring one from sin,
That voice from heaven reclaimed again.

And many passed it coldly by,
And knew not that the loved were nigh,
And said, "It is an evil thing
To listen to the songs she sings;
Her words are full of error; go
Not in her path, it leads to woe!"

But still she swerved not from her path,
She heeded not the world's dark wrath;
But where the voice said, go, she went,
Upon her holy mission bent.
Unshrinking in the stormy blast,
Calm and serene she onward passed,
To do the work the angels gave —
Poor suffering ones of earth to save.
And what to her the scoffing sneer?
Did not bright forms her pathway cheer?
And what was scandal's scorching tone?
She did not bide its blast alone.
What though the thoughtless ones might say,
The girl is mad? She kept her way;
For, all the sneers and scorn of worlds,
Anathemas upon her hurled,
Were *nothing* in the brimming cup
That angel hands were filling up.
Could she forget that Living Tomb?
That deep, wild agony and gloom?
Could she forget her wildest prayer —
To truly live — no matter where —
So that her life, *not all in vain,*
Might homeward turn to God again?

And will she waver now? Though scorn
May meet her gaze, and though the thorn
May pierce her feet, and bind her head,
While light for *others'* paths she sheds?
While guardian angels ever near,
Are speaking words of glorious cheer,
And giving strength for every hour,
Drawn from the Father's mighty power?
No, never! Onward is her way —
The path leads to eternal day!
'Tis only when she sees how *small*
Her power to raise when others fall,
How weak *she* stands in sight of Heaven,
With all the gifts that God has given,
That she *can* falter. Only then.
An hour, and she is strong again,
Uplifted by her faith in laws
That give *effect* to every *cause*,
Proportioned to itself. Each thought,
And word and act with love that's fraught,
Each seed thus sown, at last must bloom,
Surviving e'en the darkest tomb.
Strong? Yes, *how strong! Too slight* a thing
Is human scorn the heart to sting,
When borne for Truth, and God, and Love,
When guarded by his Hosts above!

Oh, may her soul be ever strong
To triumph over pain and wrong!
No sin to dim the heavenly light
That now illumes her pathway bright;

But ever listening to the strain
That Angels sing again, again;
And ear as open to the cry
That sorrow makes in passing by.
With hand as ready to relieve,
And *even more*, than to receive;
And soul out flowing in its love,
To that bright host in Heaven above;
And unto God, the mighty Giver —
In deeds of love, in high endeavor —
The soul's true offering forever!

CPSIA information can be obtained
at www.ICGtesting.com
Printed in the USA
LVHW022010120422
716028LV00006B/242

9 783752 590425